Table

Chapter One
Chapter Two
Chapter Three
Chapter Four
Chapter Five
Chapter Six
Chapter Seven
Chapter Eight
Author's Notes

CHAPTER ONE

"Good morning, Hector."

Those three words were all California's Senate candidate Hector Esteban needed to hear as he walked into his bedroom to know that he was going to die. It wasn't so much the words, as the person saying them. Seeing Sara sitting in the chair alongside his bed with the handgun pointed at his chest merely confirmed that belief.

The four men he'd sent to kill her had failed. The perimeter walls surrounding the house, the alarm system, the armed guards at the gate, the guards patrolling the grounds, and the two security men on patrol in the car around the house had all failed to stop her, and now he was going to die.

"I'll bet you're surprised to see me here," said Sara coldly as she kept her handgun pointed at his chest. "No doubt you thought Victor and his brothers would be having some fun with me about now. Would you like to tell me why you sent those four thugs to kill me, or should I just deal with this now?"

Hector stood frozen at the foot of the bed. His mind frantically raced through every available option and they all seemed inadequate. There was no place to run to, there was no place to hide, and there was no one to help him. This bedroom had always been a sanctuary to him, but now it was a trap. He could call out for his security people, but he'd be dead before they could intervene. He was trapped and he was going to die here.

He'd spent the last six hours downstairs in his office waiting to hear back from the Mazza brothers that the job had been done. His attempts to reach them had been fruitless. By three in the morning, he'd finally concluded they must have finished the job and he decided to go to bed. Now he knew that they'd failed. Not only had they failed, but they'd given him up in the process.

Hector looked to where his wife was lying in bed and noticed she had an IV in her right arm. He checked to be sure she was still breathing before speaking.

"Is Carol okay?"

"She's fine. Your kids and their nanny are also fine. I've just sedated them so they're not a part of our little reunion. They'll wake up in a few hours and have no memory of what happened here. Or, I could kill them like I did Gabrielle. It all depends on what happens in the next few minutes."

Hector looked at Sara and thought that she looked much like she had when he had first met her a few years ago. Her hair was darker, a bit longer and her face was a bit more drawn, but she was still very attractive. She'd changed clothes from the start of the night. The Mazza brothers had sent him a photo of her being picked up for her date earlier to confirm her identity and she'd been wearing a short blue dress then, not the black pants and top she wore now.

Hector's marriage to Gabrielle had proven to be a colossal failure. Whatever passion there had been between the two had long ago died. His relationship with Carol, who had been serving as a campaign adviser for him in a local race, had already advanced to a place where something had to be done. They were spending too much time together to keep their relationship a secret for much longer. He knew that Gabrielle was getting suspicious and it was only a matter of time until she would demand answers.

Divorcing Gabrielle would have been too costly, both politically and financially. Gabrielle knew enough of his past to destroy his political future, making a divorce impossible. He'd become a laughingstock, lose custody of his kids, and even possibly face imprisonment if Gabrielle turned against him, and Gabrielle had made it clear that a clean break was out of the question. A colleague had heard of his issue and referred him to Sara.

While Hector was off on a campaign trip, Sara had entered the house and dispatched Gabrielle in a manner that made her death appear natural. Their maid had found Gabby lying in bed the next morning after she had died in her sleep. A brief investigation showed no signs of foul play and the death was quickly ruled natural. Only Hector and Sara knew the whole truth. After a brief mourning period, Hector and Carol had gone public and married soon afterward.

"Do you remember that warning I gave you when we met to arrange Gabrielle's death?"

Hector nodded and replied, "You said you'd make my life a living hell if I ever sent anyone after you."

"And what did you do? You sent four thugs after me just a few years later. As you can now see, I don't make idle threats."

"Is there anything I can do to make this all go away? I don't have a lot of money here, but I can come up with some."

"This isn't about money Hector."

Hector laughed out loud and was rewarded with a look of genuine surprise on Sara's face.

"This isn't about getting money? Your boyfriend shows me your picture at the gym and you're not here to shake me down? Come on! Give me some credit for God's sake! I'm not a moron. You're shaking me down. You might as well admit it. Just name your price. You want something. What is it?"

"Kevin showed you my picture?"

"You know he did. He came up to me in the gym this morning going on and on about this girl he was dating. He was baiting me to ask to see a photo and when I did, there you were. Just tell me what you want."

"Hector, Hector, Hector," said Sara as she slowly shook her head and raised the pistol upwards. "I thought you were smarter than that. Think about it for a minute. You have some idea of the people I've worked for. If I was going to blackmail someone, would it be you? You don't have one-tenth of the money of some of my other clients."

Hector stared at Sara for a few seconds as his brain slowly processed what she'd said. Indeed, he had referred a man to her who was far wealthier than he was and there were rampant rumors that she'd handled clients even wealthier than that on some occasions. Some of her clients were also far more powerful than he was.

"But, the photo?" muttered Hector.

"It was a coincidence. I moved out here last month. I've liked it here when I've been working out here. The weather's nice, though I could live without the earthquakes. I'm thinking of getting out of the business and starting a normal life and I thought I'd like to live here. I met Kevin in a local grocery store. We've been dating for a few weeks. There was nothing sinister about it. Your paths just crossed. Did Kevin ask you for money?"

"No. So, you're not here to blackmail me?"

"I don't play that game. I've got enough money. If I was here to blackmail you, you'd know it. I'm not the most subtle girl in the world."

"What happens now?" asked Hector thinking for the first time that he might live through this.

"The answer to that is largely up to you. You're going to have to convince me that I can trust you not to send anyone else after me, or I'll have to deal with this here and now. I don't want to spend the rest of my life wondering if more of your thugs are going to try and get the jump on me."

"I swear to God I won't send anyone else after you!"

"Call me crazy, but I wonder if you'd be saying that if I wasn't sitting here with a gun pointed at you. It's amazing how a little thing like having a gun pointed at someone can change their mind, but the change is often only temporary. I need to know that when my gun isn't pointed at you that you'll still feel the same way."

"I thought you were shaking me down, that's the only reason I sent those guys after you," explained Hector frantically. There was a chance he was going to live through this and he had to make sure he didn't throw that chance away. If there was one thing Hector was good at, it was telling people whatever it took to get his way. "I swear it! I just freaked out when I saw your photo. I just assumed you were here to blackmail me."

"And that's why you sent those thugs after me?"

"I had to do something to stop word of my role in Gabrielle's death from leaking out. If word of that came out, I could lose the election. Even without proof, just the allegation could cost me enough votes to make me lose. If I'd known this wasn't an attempt to blackmail me, I would have never sent them after you. You've got to believe me!"

Sara stared at Hector for a minute or two before raising the gun and nodding.

"Okay. I believe you. As long as you don't send any more thugs after me you can just go back to normal. However, I'm afraid your little games have complicated my life. The bodies of your four thugs are now littering the area and there's no guarantee that they can't be traced back to me, so I've got to leave the area."

"You killed the Mazza brothers?"

"They didn't give me any other option. They tried to ambush us in an alley. I was able to disarm one of them and turn that weapon on the others. Two dropped their weapons and complied, but the other one refused, so I had to kill him. Then I needed to know who had sent them and the other three weren't especially forthcoming, at least not initially. It took a bit of, shall we say convincing, to get the information I needed. Once I had the information I needed, I got rid of them. They wouldn't have been a lot of good for you in the shape they were in.

"They also struck me as the type to carry a grudge. Even if I disappeared, Kevin has roots in the area and he's staying here. Unfortunately, I'm afraid I had to show Kevin a bit more of my true self than I was planning to for us to both be safe tonight, so that relationship is over."

"Did you kill him too?" asked Hector briefly wondering exactly how many people Sara had killed in her life.

"Kevin? No. Kevin's a really good guy. It took me forever to find one. There aren't that many good guys around, I'm not about to kill one of them. He's currently sedated and in his apartment while I resolve this part of the issue, but sometime this morning he should wake up. He witnessed much of what went down with the Mazza brothers though and I'm afraid he might be a tad traumatized. He had to step out and vomit a few times when things got intense. I'm quite sure he'll never look at a pair of pliers the same way again. Oh, and by the way, I think you've lost his vote. He was solidly behind you, but then when he heard that the guys who were trying to kill us were sent by you, he decided he liked the other guy more. Sorry about that."

"I can't have him telling people about this," said Hector.

"He won't tell anyone. I've warned him of the consequences. He's seen what I'm capable of. He'll keep what happened last night a secret. It will no doubt haunt him for a bit, but there's not much I can do about that."

"You're asking me to trust him a lot," said Hector. "My career depends on what happened with Gabrielle being kept secret."

"Let me make this clear. If anything happens to Kevin, then I'm holding you responsible. If he catches a cold, it's your fault. If he stumbles and falls down a staircase, I'll assume you were responsible. I want nothing bad to happen to him. He's a good guy who just found himself in the wrong place at the wrong time, largely because of the actions you took. I think I've proven my ability to overcome your best defenses, so unless you want me showing up here again then leave Kevin alone. If you don't want to go along with that, then I can just deal with this now. It's not that big of a problem for me either way."

"I don't want to die. I'll do whatever you ask."

Sara smiled for a second before asking, "Who said you would die?"

"I assumed you were going to kill me?"

"Killing you was never in the plans," laughed Sara. "I had other plans if this went badly."

"What other plans?"

"There are plenty of ways to destroy someone without killing them. If you take away everything they love, then you can destroy them more effectively than by killing them. In your case, I could have killed Carol, your kids, and the nanny. I could have left a trail of evidence that pointed to you as the killer. I could have made it look like you'd raped the nanny and one or both of your kids before killing them. I could have even pinned the deaths of the Mazza brothers on you. It would be child's play to set you up.

"I could have made it so easy for the jury that they'd have no choice but to convict you. Even the OJ jury would convict you based on the evidence I could leave behind. You'd spend the rest of your life alone, in prison, and be a target for every bad guy in the system. You'd lose everything. You'd lose your job, your status, your wife, your kids, they would all be gone. All you'd be is an empty shell living out a lot of empty years in prison. It's a far more effective way of dealing with these matters than just killing someone. People can die quickly. I prefer to make those who have wronged me suffer for a long, long time."

Hector glanced down once more at his wife and thought of his children and their nanny. He then imagined the headlines that would accompany them being found both abused and murdered in his home with all of the evidence pointing towards him. Just the thought of losing Carol and the children was enough to bring a chill to his body, and the thought of being held responsible for their deaths was unimaginable.

"I don't want that. Leave my family alone and I'll do anything you want."

"Then be a good boy and nothing bad will happen. You just leave Kevin alone and don't send anyone after me again and you can forget I ever existed."

"I won't come after you. I won't go after Kevin. I don't even have anyone else left now that you've killed the Mazza brothers. They were the ones who did this type of thing for me."

"You may not have noticed this, but there are a lot of armed guys guarding this house. They strike me as being both capable and willing to engage in some less than legal activity."

"They're from Carol's father's security firm. I don't control them, he does. They're here to keep Carol and the kids safe more than me." Hector glanced down at Carol once more and wondered how his father-in-law would react if he saw his daughter lying in bed like this. He was sure he wouldn't be happy, and the thought of Roger Bentley getting angry with him was not comforting.

"So, we're good then?" asked Hector.

"We're far from good, but I don't see a need to escalate matters as long as you don't come after me again and you leave Kevin alone."

"I've learned my lesson."

"We'll see. Actions will speak louder than words. I'll be keeping my eyes on you. Send anyone after me, or harm Kevin in any way, and there'll be hell to pay."

"I swear to you, I'll never come after you again!"

"It's time you went to sleep then."

"I don't know if I can," said Hector honestly. Despite the now early hour, sleep was the farthest thing from his mind. There was more adrenalin flowing through his body than he would have dreamt possible earlier. "I don't know if I can sleep for a week after this."

Sara removed a vial of clear liquid from her pocket and said, "You'll sleep. Now change into whatever you sleep in and do what you would normally do before bed."

Hector removed his clothes and folded them and put them away as he would normally and then pulled on his pajamas. When he was done he looked to Sara who nodded for him to lie in the bed alongside his wife. When he was in place she handed him the small vial.

"Drink this."

"What is it?" asked Hector nervously.

"It's a sedative that will knock you out while I retrieve my stuff and get out of here. It's the same stuff everyone else here has already taken. You'll wake up refreshed and ready for battle tomorrow, well later today now."

"And everyone will be fine? My wife and kids will be fine?"

"I don't kill for fun, or without a reason. They'll be fine. They'll wake up well-rested and ready to go."

Hector stared at the vial of clear liquid and wondered if he'd wake up. He was about to discuss the issue more, but glancing at Sara he saw that she was growing impatient. He knew he had no alternative so he opened his mouth and poured the liquid in. He handed back the empty vial. There was little taste to the liquid and it almost seemed to turn into a mist as he poured it in. There was little doubt in his mind of its effectiveness though. Almost immediately he could feel his eyelids starting to get heavy.

Sara picked up something from the table alongside her and held it before Hector. He tried to focus on it but his focus was less than ideal.

"This is a video camera that belonged to the Mazza brothers and I've got their confessions and admissions on it along with everything you've said here tonight. Send anyone after me ever again, and this video goes public. Do you understand?"

"What?" muttered Hector as he stared at the blurry image of the camera. He reached forward to grab it, but the room seemed to swirl around him and then all went black.

"You big dummy," muttered Sara as she arranged Hector's body into a relatively normal sleeping position and then pulled the covers up over him. She removed the IV from Carol's arm and applied pressure over the injection site to minimize any possible bruising. Carol stirred briefly from the pressure on her arm and tried to pull away, but the sedation was still strong enough to keep her just semi-conscious. Sara repacked her equipment and then briefly checked on the condition of the kids and nanny before leaving the house.

* * *

Hector woke up to see Carol finishing getting dressed and moving around the room.

"It's about time you woke up," said Carol. "I thought you were going to sleep the whole day away."

"What time is it?" asked Hector groggily.

"It's almost nine. I was letting you sleep. You've worked yourself to exhaustion."

"Are you okay?"

"Me? I'm fine. I slept like a log last night."

Hector sat on the edge of the bed and rubbed his eyes. Had it all happened, or was it just a dream? He watched as Carol put in her earrings and then he saw the small red spot on her right forearm. It hadn't been a dream.

"What happened to your arm?" asked Hector pointing at the small red spot.

Carol looked down to where he motioned and said, "I don't know. I think something bit me. It's nothing."

"Are the kids okay?"

"They're down playing their video games. Stephanie's watching them. Are you okay? Did you drink too much last night? You look hung over."

"I only drank a little, but I feel hung over. It was a long night."

"What was going on anyway? You seemed tense yesterday. Was it the polling numbers?"

"It's just everything was kind of piling up yesterday. I think it's all okay though."

"Of course, it's okay! You've got this election wrapped up. Dad's working on getting you some more funding and the party is solidly behind you. You're going to be the next senator and you'll do great. But now, you've got to get up and get out there campaigning."

Hector smiled at Carol and looked out the window. It was cloudy and overcast, but it was the most beautiful day he'd ever seen. Everyone was alive and well and right now that mattered more than anything else.

"It's a beautiful day!" said Hector.

Carol turned around and looked at him for a minute before shaking her head and leaving the room. "You're crazy!" she shouted back as she left.

Hector rose from the bed and shook his head to try and clear the cobwebs. A few hours ago he thought he'd be dead by now. Instead, he was alive and well, as was his family. The only negative was that there was a video of him out there that could be a problem down the road, but he had to trust Sara and assume that as long as he kept his word, that she'd do the same. Knowing the alternative, this seemed like a small price to pay.

CHAPTER TWO

Several years later.

Senator Hector Esteban looked around the conference room as the most influential members of the party took their seats at the conference table. As was true of both political parties, the most powerful people in the party were largely unknown to the general public. Some puppets were put out in front of the cameras, but the people gathered around this table ran the party. They picked the national candidates, provided the funding, and did everything possible to control the elections.

The seven men and three women sitting around this table were among the wealthiest and most powerful people in the country. However, they were largely unknown to the general public. While some with extreme wealth flaunted it and craved publicity, these men and women preferred to live in the shadows and control things from there.

Hector was confident that he knew what they were all here for. The convention was coming up and everyone in the country was speculating on who would be Eleanor Brown's vice presidential nominee. He knew that he was under consideration and had reason to believe he was the front runner. His father-in-law, Roger Bentley, the founder of Bentley Security, sat at the head of the table and opened the conversation.

"Senator Esteban," started Roger calmly. "I know you think we're here to offer you the vice presidency. I'm afraid that's not going to happen."

Hector tried to hide his disappointment as he nodded his head solemnly and wondered where this was all going.

"What I'm about to tell you is for your ears only. As you know, Eleanor fought a grueling campaign to win the nomination. For the last month, she was feeling tired and worn down. Everyone had assumed it was the stress of the campaign that was taking a toll on her. A few days ago she underwent a complete physical and learned that it wasn't the campaign that was taking a toll on her. Eleanor has a large, inoperable, malignant tumor. I'm afraid her time with us is to be measured in weeks, or at best months. Because of that, the party has had to scramble a bit concerning the nomination.

"We've consulted with her about what she felt was the best move for the party for the upcoming election. As you know, she doesn't hold her former competitors in the primary in great regard, and their showing in the primaries did nothing to make any of us think they are truly viable candidates."

Indeed, thought Hector. Throughout the campaign, the press had called Eleanor's opponents the seven dwarfs. Their showing in the primary season had done nothing to change that impression. None had come close to winning even a single state thus handing Eleanor the nomination.

"Your name came up in the conversation and she strongly supported you as her replacement on the ticket. We've done some preliminary polling and you seem to be our best shot at winning the presidency. We're here to formally offer you the nomination."

Hector nodded his head and paused for a few seconds to comprehend everything before replying.

"I am truly honored," said Hector respectfully, "But, how would all of this work? Eleanor isn't officially nominated until the convention. What happens with the delegates and the other candidates?"

"Eleanor will make the announcement of her illness at the convention and pledge her delegates to you," said Roger Bentley. "Even if only fifty percent of her delegates follow through on her wishes, you'll win the nomination. The other two leading candidates, such as they are, have both been approached and are familiar with the situation. While they're not happy about not being the nominee, they understand the situation. Neither will mount a serious challenge. We'll see to that. We need a candidate to reach the independents and our polling shows you to be that candidate."

Hector knew that one of the great truths of American politics is that nationally, roughly forty percent of the people will vote Democratic regardless of the candidate and forty percent will vote Republican regardless of the candidate, leaving control of the country up to the other twenty percent. He'd always targeted that twenty percent of unaligned voters in his campaigns and had won because of it. Too many on the left reached out to only those on the left, and too many on the right reached only to the right. Neither mattered if you could get the majority of that twenty percent who were more flexible. They controlled the elections. Win the majority of the independents and you'd win the election. The diehards in both parties will vote the party line no matter what.

"We need you," said Roger Bentley, "We need a new voice. We can provide you with the funding and the help you'll need. We can guarantee you the nomination and you'll have an excellent shot at winning the presidency."

"I'm happy as a Senator. I'm doing good work."

"You could do more from the White House," said his father-in-law. "Our polling shows that you have the best chance in this coming election. We can't afford to lose the White House."

All eyes in the room were focused on Hector as he spoke. "I'm honored. Truly, I am. But I can't make this type of decision without consulting with my wife and family. There are a lot of things that need to be considered. Thank you all for this opportunity, but I'm going to have to think about this for a while."

The group rose and disbanded. Everyone but his father-in-law left the room. Roger Bentley carried over two glasses of scotch and handed one to Hector before sitting down alongside him.

"You handled that well. You came across as thoughtful and careful. Carol said you had greatness ahead of you and by God she was right."

"I don't know about this Roger. I'm not sure I want to put myself and my family through this kind of campaign. Some things weren't an issue in my Senate campaigns that might come out in a presidential campaign."

"There's nothing that can come up that we can't handle," said Roger confidently. "Is there anything specific that's troubling you?"

Hector paused for a long time before answering. He wasn't sure how his father-in-law would respond to what he was about to say, but it was better to hear it from Hector than to have it break on its own.

"Gabrielle. Her death might be brought up."

"She died of heart failure. What can they make of that?"

"Suppose it wasn't a natural death?"

"What are you saying?"

"I arranged for Gabrielle to die," said Hector quietly. "There's a woman who performed that service for me."

"Is she trying to blackmail you?"

"No. She isn't. I misunderstood a situation back when I was first running for the Senate. I thought I was being set up by her and some guy she was with. I sent some guys after her. She killed them and came after me and could have killed me, but we made a deal. I promised not to send anyone else after her and she let me live. She made a video of our conversation where I admitted to hiring her to kill Gabby. If that video came out…"

"And you're worried that if you ran for the presidency it might come out?"

"Can you imagine a bigger incentive? I can't afford to have someone holding something like that over me. As long as that video exists there's the real threat of it being used against me, either to derail my campaign or commandeer the presidency."

Both men sat in silence for several minutes before the father-in-law spoke.

"What happened to Gabrielle?"

Hector paused for a few seconds before answering.

"Gabrielle and I had met in college, fallen in love, and gotten married. In later years we'd grown apart. She was proving to be a burden. I couldn't keep her happy. She was spending money at an insane rate. We'd lost whatever feelings we'd had for each other. As much as anything we were staying together for the kids, but there was no real relationship left. I had met Carol and we'd become close. I wanted to separate from Gabrielle to be with Carol.

"We didn't have a prenup so I stood to lose half of everything if I divorced Gabrielle. There would have been some major political damage too. Gabrielle knew stuff about me that no one else knew that could have been damaging if it had come out."

"What did she know that could damage your career?"

"There were guys I'd hired to handle some of the messier parts of running for office. They were some local thugs who would do dirty work for me. She knew the details of what they'd done. She'd grown up with them and that's how I met them. They were more loyal to her than me. If she leaked that information, things could have gotten ugly.

"I would have likely lost custody of the kids and had no political future. I could have even ended up in jail. She made it clear that there would be no clean break. I was her money source and she wasn't going to let me off easy. She had access to a hundred percent of my income while we were married, and God knows she was using most of it, and if we divorced she'd only get fifty percent. A friend told me about this woman who could fix the problem for me. I contacted her and we met. We made a deal, I paid the money, and Gabrielle died of heart failure shortly after that."

"Do you know for a fact that this woman killed her?"

"Yes. The woman I'd hired had me give her a copy of the house key and the alarm code. She waited until I was out of town and thus not a suspect then entered the house and killed Gabby in a manner to make the death appear natural."

"The video you mentioned? Do you have a copy of the video?"

"No."

"It shows you talking to this woman?"

"Yes. I pretty much confess to everything during the conversation."

Roger Bentley sighed and sat back in the chair for a few seconds pondering the situation before speaking.

"We've got to resolve this. Come to my house tomorrow evening. I'll have someone there who can help you. You're not to talk about this to anyone else. Does Carol know?"

"No. We had been seeing each other for a while at the time, but she played no part in this. As far as she knows Gabrielle's death was a stroke of good luck that allowed our relationship to move out into the open. She knows nothing about all of this."

"Keep it that way. Is that the only reason you're reluctant to run?"

"Do I need more?"

"We'll sort this out pretty quickly. We'll find the girl, get the video, and end this threat. It won't stop you from running and winning. I'll talk to you tomorrow. Don't worry about this. Problem will disappear. I've dealt with bigger issues in the past."

* * *

Hector showed up at his father-in-law's house early the next evening and was escorted into the library where Roger was waiting with another man. This was a room that exuded power. The beautiful wood-paneled walls, the leather-bound books filling the shelves, the carpeting that one sank into, and the scent of cigar smoke that lingered in the air, all combined to give an illusion of power. This was the room of a rich and powerful man. That rich and powerful man now rose from behind the desk to greet Hector.

"This is Craig Burke," said Roger nodding to the other man in the room. "He heads up a special unit of my security operations. I've given him a brief overview of your situation and he's confident he can fix this problem of yours. I've got an event that I have to attend, so I'm going to leave you two alone. I want you to tell him everything and answer his every question. Craig is one hundred percent trustworthy and discreet. Nothing said here will ever leave this room."

"Senator Esteban," said Craig offering his hand to Hector as Roger left the room.

Craig Burke looked like a man who could immediately take off his suit coat and play middle linebacker for any NFL team. He had broad shoulders, a narrow waist, and appeared to be heavily muscled, an observation that was confirmed by the strength of the handshake that greeted Hector. He also appeared to be fairly light on his feet as he moved away from Hector and took a seat. Hector took the chair opposite him and wondered how to open this conversation. Craig relieved him of that burden.

"Your father-in-law told me the basics. From what I understand, you hired a woman to kill your first wife and that person now has possession of material that could implicate you in a criminal act. Is that reasonably accurate?"

"That's about it."

"We're going to have to find her then. Do you know her name?"

"She called herself Sara X. I'm pretty sure that's not her real name."

"Can you describe her?"

"She's about five foot six inches tall, maybe weighs a hundred and thirty pounds. She's got nice features, pretty, but not intimidating looking. She had short brownish hair then."

"How did you first meet her?"

"I was referred to her by an acquaintance."

"Who referred you to her?"

"Do we have to go into that? He's a friend and I don't want to draw him into this."

"To find her, I have to know everything there is to know about her. You have had limited contact with her, so I need to find other people who have had contact with her. The more I learn about her, the easier it is to track her down. Who told you about her?"

"Josh Stafford."

"The sports agent?"

"Yes."

"How did he know her?"

"Josh had gotten involved with a young woman. She had gotten pregnant and was threatening to tell his wife. He tried to buy her off, but she wanted to take his wife's place and Josh didn't want that. He knew his wife would leave him if she found out and he couldn't afford to lose his wife. Someone told him about Sara and he hired her to do the job. The girl was found dead of natural causes a short time later. The police looked into it, but there was absolutely no evidence of a crime and the autopsy showed nothing unusual other than the pregnancy."

"Do you know who told him about her?"

"It was one of his clients, but I don't know which one. One or more of his players had used her services before. She was well known among professional athletes and had done a lot of work for them. They tend to marry young, get rich, and lose half of their money when they get divorced. They kept Sara pretty busy."

"How did you make contact with her?"

"Josh gave me an e-mail address that I could use to contact her. He advised me to buy a prepaid cellular phone and to use that phone only for conversations with her. Once I had the phone number I was to e-mail her that number and a code word he gave me. She would then contact me if she was available, or as soon as she became available. The code word would identify who had referred me. She could then check with them to see who I was."

"You followed his instructions?"

"Yes. She called me back a couple of days later. We arranged to meet at a place of her choosing."

"Where was the meeting?"

"It was in an abandoned house out in the middle of nowhere. From what Josh told me she never used the same place twice."

"What happened at the meeting?"

"She was waiting for me. She frisked me. She ran a wand over me checking for listening devices. Once she was convinced I was clean she confirmed who I was and asked what I wanted to be done. I told her. As it turned out she already knew everything. Once I was done she slid some photographs of Gabrielle over to verify her identity. She'd been observing my house and had done a background check on me. She knew just about everything there was to know about me."

"Including your relationship with Carol?"

"Yes," said Hector sheepishly. "I thought we'd been discreet, but she'd found out about us and had some photos of us together."

"What happened then?"

"She told me what she'd do and named her price."

"What was the price?"

"The price was one hundred thousand dollars."

"That's kind of pricey," said Craig.

"It's like she said, you get what you pay for, and compared to what a divorce would have cost me in legal fees alone, it was a bargain. Gabby's life insurance policy ultimately covered both the cost and her funeral expenses, so the cash wasn't a big deal."

"How did you handle the payment?"

"It was a cash deal. Josh had told me what the price was to be and I'd brought it with me. My campaign was handling a lot of money so it wasn't too hard to make a hundred thousand disappear. We had a pretty big slush fund built up that was undocumented. I took the money out of that fund. Once I got the life insurance money back I replaced it. No one was the wiser."

"How did she carry out the hit?"

"I'm not sure. From what I've heard, she injects something into the victims that will stop their hearts and it's undetectable, but I don't know what. She had me give her a copy of the house keys and the alarm code. She wanted to know about surveillance cameras. I told her all about Gabrielle's normal habits and lifestyle. Then when I was out of town on a trip, she did the job."

"Our housekeeper found Gabby the next morning looking like she was still asleep, only she wasn't breathing. She called 911 and the police and paramedics showed up pretty quickly but Gabby was gone. The police went over the house with a fine-toothed comb and checked the surveillance cameras, but nothing seemed out of the ordinary. The alarm hadn't been triggered. There was no sign of forced entry. No unexpected fingerprints were found. I was notified and immediately flew back home. They questioned me and I told them that we'd been having trouble but were trying to work through it. They were suspicious, but there was absolutely no evidence of foul play. The autopsy and toxicology reports all came back clean, so Gabby's death was written off as a natural death. She had some sedative in her system but it wasn't at a toxic level so that was largely overlooked."

"When did you see Sara again?"

"It was a couple of years later. I was in a gym talking with a guy in the next locker. We were talking about women and he was bragging about this great new girlfriend of his. He showed me her picture on his phone. It was Sara. I thought they were teaming up to blackmail me. I couldn't believe it was just a coincidence. I tried to get rid of them using some guys who did stuff like that for me. They followed the guy until he led them to her. They were just waiting for the right moment to take them out when she saw them and took control. She killed one of them, disarmed the rest, tortured them for information on who'd sent them, and then killed them before coming after me."

"What happened?"

"I was home with Carol and the kids. Carol had gone upstairs to go to bed. I was waiting to hear from the guys who were trailing her, but I finally gave up. I went upstairs and found Carol unconscious with an IV in her arm. Sara was sitting there alongside her with a gun in her hand. She denied being in town to blackmail me. She was just dating the guy and it was all a coincidence. I agreed not to send any more thugs after her and she said she would disappear. Just before leaving she had me drink something and just before I passed out she waved a camera in front of me and told me that our whole conversation was taped."

"What had you discussed?"

"I'd admitted to hiring her to kill Gabby. I admitted to sending the four guys after her. There was enough on that tape to cost me dearly. If it got out, I'd be ruined. Also, she told me that if I didn't follow through she'd kill Carol and the kids and set me up to take the blame. I'm pretty sure she would too."

"Have you had any contact with her since that time?"

"She called me once about two months after that."

"What was that about?"

"I had referred someone to her. He was having some domestic issues. She called to verify his identity and get some background on him. I wasn't sure if she was still in the business, but this guy was desperate so I thought it couldn't hurt. That was the last time I've talked to her."

"Did she take that job?"

"Yes."

"I'll need that guy's name."

Hector hesitated a few long seconds before responding. "Billy Small."

"The Governor?"

"Yes."

"That was ballsy on her part," said Craig admiringly.

"She doesn't lack for nerve."

"How did she get past the security?"

"I don't know. Billy could probably tell you that."

"We'll have to talk to him. How's your security situation now?"

"It's pretty good. We upgraded the alarm system and changed the locks and codes after Sara's last visit. Everything's been upgraded and Roger has extra security on patrol now."

"I'll have some of my guys take a look at what you've got and maybe we'll test it out to see how good it is."

"I don't know if anything can stop her. She's damned good at what she does."

"I can assure you that we can stop her. She may be good, but we're better. Once you announce your candidacy you'll pick up Secret Service protection also."

"If I announce," corrected Hector. "We've got to get this resolved first."

"We'll make this issue disappear for you. We'll track down the girl and the video and eliminate that threat. As of now, you can officially forget that any of this ever happened. I'll need that e-mail address and any other information you can give me. We'll find this girl and end this threat. It won't be a problem."

* * *

After finishing the questioning Hector left his father-in-law's house and returned to his home. Craig started the investigation and was waiting when Roger returned from his evening out.

"What did you find out?" asked Roger.

"Your son-in-law did well with his hire. The girl looks like she's a pro." He relayed the rest of the interview to Roger who interrupted at one stage of the replay.

"She drugged Carol and threatened to kill her and the kids?" asked Roger indignantly.

"That's what he told me. I take it you didn't know that?"

"No," said Roger angrily. "This bitch drugged my daughter?"

"Your daughter, the nanny, and the kids were all sedated to keep them quiet during the meeting. If things went south, it sounds like she planned to kill them and pin the blame on Hector."

"This is getting personal. I want her found and I want this threat eliminated. I also want the security around my daughter and grandchildren to be increased. I don't want this bitch getting within a mile of her again. Is that clear?"

"Yes sir. I've already got a team on the way to examine the security situation at his home. They'll be reporting back later tonight and we'll see what steps need to be taken to enhance the security situation."

* * *

For the next week, a team of investigators swept the country following trails and leads to try to find Sara X. Craig Burke had now returned to Roger Bentley's house and was advising Roger on what he'd found.

"Starting with the information we had, we were able to track her both forward and backward from the time of Hector's first contact with her. We've now been able to directly link her to thirty-nine deaths and we strongly suspect her in over fifty other cases. We're still trying to nail everything down. She gets clients almost entirely by word of mouth, so we've gone back and built a statistical model of her known clients, their contacts and relationships, and any unusual deaths among and around them that occurred in the window of time when she was active. We're probably missing a lot, but based on what we've learned it looks like she was kept very busy.

"There are months here where we have no activity at all. We suspect there are other contacts of hers referring work to her during those periods. We'll have to find one or more of them to nail it down more precisely. Statistically, anyone who has knowledge of, or contact with this girl is fifty times more likely to have someone close to them experience an unusually early, supposedly natural death. The girl is damned good.

"Her true identity has now been determined," continued Craig. "Her given name is Janet Mills. We have a pretty complete biography of her. Her parents died in a car accident while she was in college. She has no siblings or close blood relatives. She worked for a while as a phlebotomist, then on the IV team for a major teaching hospital where she got her training. She became extraordinarily proficient in hitting veins in even the smallest neonatal cases and was highly thought of by her co-workers. She'd gotten involved with a married anesthesiologist while working at the facility.

"We believe it was around then that she committed her first killing. The wife of the anesthesiologist died of an apparent heart attack while he was out of town at a convention. Janet then apparently broke off the relationship with the anesthesiologist. She'd come into a substantial amount of money in some manner as she took a very expensive vacation. When the vacation ended Janet Mills vanished. She's never used that name again. We then had a series of untimely deaths of spouses of people associated with the anesthesiologist. One was the wife of a golfing buddy who died in her sleep while the husband was out of town on a business trip. Another was the husband of an old girlfriend of the anesthesiologist who died in his sleep right after the anesthesiologist and the guy's then-wife had reunited at a class reunion. The anesthesiologist and the widow then started dating after a few weeks and got married a year later. There's quite a large group of unusual deaths that presented among those who had contact with that doctor and his contacts over the next few years."

"Did she kickback money to those guys?" asked Roger.

"It doesn't look that way. All the money went to her. They used her services and paid her a fairly substantial sum from what we can gather. Examination of the financial records of those who were likely to have hired her seems to indicate that she made around a hundred thousand per kill. We have reason to believe that in some cases she made more."

"How much money did she make during that period?"

"It's hard to say. We're figuring she probably has somewhere around thirty to forty million dollars stashed away. That number could be off by fifty percent one way or the other, but it should be in that ballpark."

"Jesus!"

"There's a spiderweb like map showing connections between suspected victims and her on one of the walls in my office. There are a lot of people somehow connected to this girl, and those who know her, that seem to lose spouses and associates on a much more frequent basis than would appear natural. A very high percentage of unexplained, seemingly natural deaths occur to those linked to this woman.

"Many of the deaths occur in someone who has a high, though a nonlethal dose of sedative in their system. It looks like she sedates them and then painlessly executes them somehow. We're not sure of the means quite yet, but the anesthesiologist she was associated with had been looking for new anesthetics when she was involved with him. We're assuming one of those drugs is what she's used. He died a year ago though so that line of inquiry is dead"

"Where is she now?"

"That's the ten thousand dollar question. She's assumed multiple identities through the years, often changing them from one week to the next and in some cases one day to the next. We've been trying to keep up with those identities to determine if there's a pattern to where she stays when she's in a town and what her habits are, but we're not making a lot of progress. There are huge holes in what we know about her as of now. We have a vague road map of her moves and activities up to five years ago when she just dropped off the map. We don't know what she's been doing in the years since then. She may be dead."

"But, you don't think she is?"

"I think she just got tired of it and quit. We know she was getting bored. She started taking on other kinds of contracts. She did a couple of jobs with a sniper rifle. One of my guys has checked out the sites and he was impressed. She must have spent quite some time practicing to get the level of precision she exhibited in those hits. She even did a couple of close-in kills using knives and handguns. She would do whatever it took to get the job done. She could get quite close to people without drawing undue attention. If she wasn't the enemy here, I'd recommend we hire her. The girl's damned good."

"Are the police actively looking for her?" asked Roger.

"No. Nearly all of the cases were ruled a natural death, with the only exceptions being the gun and knife cases. All they have in those cases are some fingerprints and they didn't match anyone on file. From what I've gathered, they weren't looking for a woman anyway. They have some eyewitness accounts of taller men dressed either in black or camouflage running from the scenes. As far as I can tell, their investigations are all dead. All they seem to have are old fingerprints and conflicting physical descriptions of various suspicious men. Nothing is pointing them towards Sara X."

"Can you find her?"

"I think so. We know how she got her various identities. We know her techniques and many of her contacts. We're now looking back five years to the time when she disappeared to try to determine what identity she might have assumed then. We've found about fifty people with false identities that were created in that period using her preferred technique that we're looking at. Twenty of them are female. I'm assuming she didn't get a sex change operation, so we're limiting our search to them. Of those twenty, twelve don't come close to matching her physical characteristics. That leaves eight. Of those eight, four are now employed in dull, drudgery-type jobs that would tend to rule them out. If I had millions of dollars stashed away, there's no way I'd be plucking chickens, or working as a hotel maid. The other four we're now checking out. Three of those are housewives who could be a match. The fourth is an unemployed actress. We've gotten a headshot of her and it doesn't match the computer-generated image we have of what Sara should look like. It's likely she's one of the three housewives or someone we've overlooked along the way."

"Can you pin down her identity?"

"We were lucky in that in some of her later work she used weapons. In those cases, the deaths were treated as homicides. We've got good fingerprints from several of those crime scenes that match up. Now we're working to gather fingerprints and photographs of the three women and compare them to the ones we have on file. We should know if one of them is the girl by tonight."

"Then what happens?"

"That's pretty much up to you."

"Then we end this."

"How?"

"We kill her. We get the video first, but then we kill her. We do to her what she's done to so many others."

"Do we have to go that far? She could be an asset to us. She's damned good at what she does."

"She drugged my daughter and threatened to kill her," said Roger coldly. "You don't do that and live."

"I can't guarantee we'll find the video."

"It won't matter. The video won't have any value with her dead. Someone needs to authenticate the video to give it credibility. You can't be prosecuted without someone authenticating the video. If it goes public, we'll have experts standing by to vouch that it is a forgery. Gabrielle died of heart failure. If the video comes out we spin it to death. It won't be a problem. We should be able to pin the creation of it on our political opponents and use it against them should it come out. We can have a video team sign an affidavit testifying that they were hired to make the video. We'll get some actors who look like Hector and Carol who will testify that they were hired to play those roles. It's better if we don't have to deal with it, but in a worst-case scenario, we can handle it."

"She could be an asset for the company. She has skills."

"When she drugged Carol and my grandchildren it became personal. I was willing to buy her off. I was willing to try to deal with her. But, you don't endanger my family. I won't tolerate that. She dies."

CHAPTER THREE

Shannon Brewer was struggling to get her three-year-old son Tyler into his jacket. As is often the case with strong-willed children, Tyler felt he knew better than his mother and didn't want to wear his jacket. As soon as she'd get one arm in a sleeve, he'd pull it out.

"Jack, you're not helping," said Shannon to her husband who was standing by the kitchen door and laughing at the scene.

"Sorry," said Jack as he moved forward and helped wrestle their son into his jacket. "I was just having too much fun watching you two."

Shannon smiled up at her husband as she finally zipped the jacket shut.

"Keep laughing and I'll let you get it on him the next time," said Shannon as she rose.

"Okay, okay, okay, I'll stop laughing. Come on. We're going to be late." He held the door open for the pair as they walked out of the house towards the driveway. Shannon frowned when she saw the car her husband had pulled out of the garage.

"I thought we were taking my car," muttered Shannon as she looked at the hulking yellow Hummer that her husband had just recently purchased and that was now idling in the driveway.

"I didn't buy this baby to keep it in the garage," said Jack as he held open the back door and helped secure Tyler in the child seat. "Besides, it's a neat vehicle and I like showing it off. It's also safer than anything else. The thing's built like a tank. There's nothing wrong with showing off a little."

"This is coming from the man who complained bitterly when his boss got a showy new car a few years ago?"

"That was different. That was a sports car. Those things aren't practical. They're just for show."

"And this is practical?"

"Sure!" said Jack happily as he climbed behind the driver's wheel. "We get twenty some inches of snow a year. This baby can plow right through that."

"We don't get all twenty inches of snow at once," reminded Shannon.

"If we ever do, then we're ready, besides it was used and cheap. This baby would have cost nearly a hundred grand brand new and I got it for less than a tenth of that."

Shannon frowned and grabbed hold of the handgrips and pulled herself into the passenger seat and buckled her seat belt.

"I swear this thing gets bigger every time I see it," muttered Shannon over the roar of the engine.

"You know what they say, bigger is better."

Jack shifted the Hummer into gear and the car moved out of the driveway and onto the road. Shannon settled back in her seat after taking a glance back at Tyler. He loved the big car and was happily kicking at the back of the driver's seat as Jack drove. Shannon closed her eyes and despite the noise from the engine and Jack's humming, she was soon drifting off to sleep.

Shannon awoke to an impact and the impassioned cursing of her husband as the Hummer bounced to a stop a hundred yards off the road.

"What happened?" asked Shannon looking around in confusion.

"Some idiot came out of nowhere and ran me off the road. There he is. I'm going to give him a piece of my mind!"

Jack jumped from the car and walked back across the field to where several vehicles had stopped. Shannon checked on Tyler who seemed unhurt and then turned to look towards where her husband was going.

In an instant, her senses were on maximum alert. Something wasn't right. It took her less time to sense the problem than it did to analyze it. She soon realized that the makeup of the people on the shoulder of the road was all wrong. Five nearly identical vehicles had stopped and there were ten men, all fit and well-dressed lining up along the shoulder. The five cars were spaced to prevent the Hummer from getting back out to the road. This wasn't an accident. This was an ambush.

"Jack!" she called out to her husband who was now halfway to the group of people. He paused, looked back briefly, and gave her a wave before continuing towards the men.

Shannon looked back at the group and saw their spacing. She also noticed that all were hiding at least one hand and were wearing heavier than expected coats for this time of year. Even though her husband was approaching the group, they were still focused almost exclusively on the Hummer. Four of the men had now started to move towards the Hummer, still keeping their hands inside their coats. Shannon undid her seat belt, hopped over the center console and into the driver's seat. She quickly buckled herself in and then shifted the Hummer into gear. She mashed the gas pedal and was soon racing towards her husband who had stopped and turned to see what she was doing. As Shannon approached him, she saw the men open their coats and remove automatic weapons from where they'd been hiding them. Shannon hurried to try to get the vehicle between the men and her husband, but she was too late. The men opened fire and Shannon saw her husband fall as bullets started to impact the vehicle.

Shannon ducked, turned the car into a hard spin, and mashed the gas pedal. The tires dug into the soft earth and the Hummer sped away from the shooters as more bullets impacted it. Shannon felt a burning pain in her right shoulder as she drove across the field and into the nearby woods. This was a new growth forest where the trees were little more than overgrown weeds. The largest, though twenty or more feet tall, were only two to three inches in diameter and were no match for the mass of the Hummer at full speed. Shannon plowed her way through the forest and came out on an old dirt road a few seconds later. She spun the truck onto the dirt road and floored the gas pedal. Blood was staining the front of her blouse and she could feel it oozing from the wound. She quickly turned the vehicle right onto a paved road and started to head back towards town.

Shannon looked behind her at Tyler and was heartbroken to see her son lying strapped in his car seat with much of his head missing. One glance was all she needed to know he was dead. All emotion left her. She became cold and empty. She wasn't sure if the coldness came from physical or emotional shock, but Shannon changed at that moment. The wife and mother had died. She had one goal now. She would find and kill those who had done this to her family. As she drove she pulled out her cell phone and threw it from the window. They could use that to track her if they didn't have any other means of tracking the vehicle. The Hummer was anything but inconspicuous too. She'd need a new vehicle and she'd need it soon.

Shannon kept watch in the rearview mirror and was almost more alarmed to see no one following her. The people who'd attacked her were pros. If they weren't following her then they must be tracking her. Up ahead of her was a convenience store with a gas station. She shopped there fairly regularly and it had never failed to amaze her how many people left their cars running while they went inside. Today her very life might depend on someone doing just that.

Shannon parked the Hummer at the far end of the parking lot and hurried towards the line of cars that were parked in front of the store. She found a black pick-up truck with the engine running and the doors unlocked. There was a gun rack with two hunting rifles behind the driver's seat. Shannon slid open the truck door, hopped in, and shifted it into gear. She raced from the store. There was a sister store to this one just a few miles away. Shannon hurried to that store and examined the cars in that lot. A man driving a small sports car pulled in and hopped out leaving the car idling.

While Shannon watched, the man walked over towards the deli section of the store. Shannon knew it would take several minutes for him to get waited on and then return to his car. She took the keys from the truck's ignition, found the key that unlocked the rifles, and grabbed the hunting rifles from the gun rack. She hurried to the sports car with the rifles and drove from the store.

Shannon knew where she had to go. There was only one place that might still be safe. Her home would not be safe, but in planning for just this type of contingency, Shannon had bought a small hunting cabin in the nearby woods. There was a lake that would swallow the car and she had supplies stashed in the cabin. She'd paid cash for the cabin and there was no paper trail showing that she owned it. Anyone looking for her would have to be extremely lucky to stumble upon her there.

* * *

Craig Burke and his men were not having a good day. Having found Shannon and verifying that she was the woman they'd wanted, they'd tagged the vehicles at her house and were tracking them. The tree-lined field they'd chosen for the confrontation was perfect. There was limited road access and his men could prevent the vehicle from escaping. The road had been blocked in both directions eliminating anyone else from witnessing the action.

The plan was simple; they'd force the Hummer from the road, grab the occupants, clean the scene and depart. No one would know they'd been there.

The operation had initially gone much as planned. They'd managed to force the Hummer off the road at the correct spot. The Hummer had come to rest farther off the road than he would have preferred, but it was within the limits. The supporting vehicles had been positioned properly. He'd expected both adults to exit the vehicle and was disappointed to find only the husband coming towards them. Even that had been okay as the planning had anticipated this possibility. The four men assigned to react in this case had awaited the signal from Craig before acting. Immediately upon getting it, they'd started moving towards the Hummer. It was then that things started to go badly.

Shannon's taking the wheel of the vehicle had been a surprise. They were forced to act before they were ready. The team that was moving to get Shannon and the kid from the Hummer found themselves caught between positions. They were in the line of fire of the other six men. When the men in their original positions opened fire, those who had been moving towards Shannon had to drop and take cover. As she drove away they were finally able to rise and join in the attack, but it was too late by then.

The ambush hadn't taken into account the ability of the Hummer to plow through the woods. His men had initially chased the vehicle on foot, sure that it would get trapped in the woods. It wasn't until they found the dirt road that they had to regroup and race back to their vehicles. Even then they were less than three minutes behind Shannon at the convenience store.

A crowd had started to gather around the Hummer when Craig's group pulled in. The bullet-wracked car with the dead child in the back was drawing a lot of attention. One of Craig's men confirmed that Shannon wasn't in the car, but that there was a substantial amount of blood in the driver's seat.

It was while getting this information that the driver of the black pickup truck first noticed it was missing. One of Craig's men quickly got the license number and a description of the truck. The cars split up and started to search for the pickup. They found it shortly afterward at the second convenience store where another customer was standing in the parking lot waiting for the police to show up and take a report concerning his stolen car. They quickly got a description and were back on the road, but to no avail. The car had disappeared. It had no tracking device in it. The car and the girl were gone.

Back at Shannon's house, the team that had entered after Shannon had left was still searching for the video when word reached them of the foul-up. Nothing incriminating had been found. No safe had been found. The hard drives had been removed from the computers. The search of the house and the outbuildings was only half done when the order came to destroy the place. Kerosene was dumped into every room of the house and the surrounding outbuildings. The last man out dropped a match and in seconds every building in the compound was ablaze.

Craig, using a scrambled phone, called in the results and took the anticipated verbal beating. He then dispatched teams to every location they could think of to find and kill Shannon. Hospitals, physician's offices, emergency rooms, homes of family and friends in the area were all put under observation, but to no avail. Shannon Brewer had disappeared. Airports, bus terminals, train stations, all were checked, but no one matching Shannon's description had passed through. Videotapes from all of the toll roads and bridges in the area had been examined, but the car had not passed. The girl had vanished into thin air along with the car she'd stolen.

* * *

Sheriff Tommy Underwood had been having a normal day. His biggest worry had been finding someone to cover for Mrs. Cahill, the elementary school crossing guard who had called in sick that morning, and then things had taken a dramatic turn.

The first call from the convenience store about a shot-up yellow Hummer with a dead child in the back had scared him to death. The only vehicle like that he'd ever seen was the one that belonged to his good friend and golfing buddy Jack Brewer and his wife Shannon. He managed to convince himself as he raced to the store that it couldn't be them. When he pulled into the parking lot, his heart sank as he saw the license plate.

The crowd around the vehicle moved back as he pulled in and parked his patrol car. One man came rushing towards him complaining that his truck had been stolen. The sheriff briefly listened to his complaint and then hurried to the Hummer. A glance in the back showed the dead son of his friend. It looked like there were a hundred bullet holes in the vehicle.

The sight of the dead child had chilled the sheriff. He backed away from the vehicle and was lost as to his next move. The man whose truck had been stolen then came back and stood in front of him.

"Sheriff, she took my truck!" said the man.

"Who?" asked the sheriff.

"I didn't see who it was, but someone here said it was a woman who got out of the SUV. They said she was hurt and ran over to my truck and took it! I need my truck!"

"Let me call for some help," said the sheriff shakily. "This is too big for me to handle alone. I want everybody to stay away from the vehicle. Don't anyone touch it! If you've already touched it, then hang around. We'll need to get your prints so if they show up when the truck is dusted we won't be looking at you as a suspect. Anyone who saw anything, stay here! No one leaves here until we've had a chance to talk to everyone."

The sheriff climbed into his patrol car and radioed in the situation to the dispatcher and asked for the state police to be dispatched to help handle the situation. He also issued the stolen truck information with a warning to approach it cautiously if found. While talking on the radio he noticed his cell phone. He finished his radio call and then picked up the cell phone. Jack Brewer's home and cellular numbers were programmed into his phone. He called the cellular number and got the voice mail. He left a message for Jack to call him as soon as possible. He then tried the home number and got no answer. While trying that number three additional calls came in over the radio. One was a fire call for the Brewer's house. The second call was for a man's body found a few miles from their home. Sheriff Underwood had little doubt whose body that would be. The third call was for another stolen car a few miles from his current location.

"What the hell is going on here?" muttered the sheriff as he climbed from the car to start interviewing the witnesses.

The witnesses were remarkably consistent in their stories. Based on the description of the witness who had seen the woman, the sheriff had little doubt it was Shannon. One odd note was the vehicles that had stopped and the man who had briefly questioned people before departing. Most had failed to mention it initially, but once one witness reported it, the others quickly confirmed the information.

The sheriff was never happier to see anyone than he was when the first state police cruiser pulled into the parking lot. This was followed in short order by four more cruisers. He turned over his information to the state police and then excused himself to go and check on the body that had been found.

One of his deputies and two state troopers were guarding the scene along with the passerby who had spotted the body lying in the field. There were tire tracks everywhere and what looked like hundreds of bullet casings. He could tell from the shoulder of the road that the body was that of his friend, Jack Brewer. His body had multiple gunshot wounds and his eyes stared vacantly up into the clouds. There was no doubt that he was dead.

"Good morning, sheriff," said the lead state trooper.

"It was until a half-hour ago," replied Sheriff Underwood. "Any idea what happened here?"

"It looks like a war broke out. Our only witness came along after the fact and saw the body and called it in. He didn't see anyone around. I'm waiting for a forensics team to come in and go over the scene. I'm afraid of trampling evidence if I go in now. There are tire tracks we should be able to get some good impressions from to say nothing of hundreds of shell casings and even some shoe impressions. Whatever happened here was pretty serious."

"Skidmarks?" asked the sheriff nodding to where the trooper and deputy had put some cones out to guide traffic around the marks.

"Yes. They look fresh and tie into one of the sets of tire tracks in the field. If you follow the skid marks onto the grass, you can see an area where it looks like someone skidded into the field. They pretty quickly straightened it out, but those tracks then go into the field. My best guess is someone forced a vehicle off the road and then opened fire on them."

"More like a pretty large group of people," said the deputy looking at the shell casings.

"I understand you found a vehicle with a lot of bullet holes?" asked the trooper.

"Yes. We found it a couple of miles from here. It used to be his," said the sheriff nodding towards where his friend lay dead in the field. "It appears his wife was driving it and she dumped it there and took some guy's truck. We had another car stolen a few miles from there. It looks like she traded the stolen truck in for a car there. None of this makes a lot of sense."

"You knew this guy?"

"Yes, I had dinner with them a couple of nights ago. They were friends and they were good people. I don't understand this."

"No drug connections, mob connections?"

"They were clean," said the sheriff. "They didn't drink, smoke, use drugs, or even gamble. Both were churchgoers and the nicest people you ever wanted to meet. This makes no sense at all. Why would someone target them?"

"How long have you known them?"

"I grew up with Jack. We were friends forever. He didn't deserve this."

"What about his wife?"

"Shannon was the perfect wife and mother. She moved into the area a while back, maybe five years ago. I did a perfunctory check on her when she started dating Jack and there was nothing in her background to suggest any problems. I just don't understand this."

"Did she have an angry ex-husband?"

"No. She'd never been married. This doesn't make any sense at all."

"Does that fire tie into this also?" asked the trooper nodding to the column of smoke that was rising in the distance.

"It looks like it," said the sheriff. "That's their house and outbuildings burning. From the calls I've heard, it doesn't look like anything is going to be left."

"It looks like someone was trying to send them a pretty clear message."

* * *

That message had been received loud and clear by Shannon Brewer. She'd driven the stolen car into the lake and entered her secluded cabin. After locking the door she made her way to the cabinet of medical supplies. She was getting fairly light-headed from the loss of blood and she knew her survival depended on her ability to treat her wound. She removed her blouse and stood in front of the mirror and briefly examined the wound. The bullet had gone clean through which was a relief to Shannon. The entry and exit wounds were fairly clean. No arteries had been hit, and even though there was a lot of pain, she was fairly certain no bones had been broken.

The loss of blood had lowered her blood pressure enough that the bleeding had slowed to a trickle, mostly from the torn skin. She quickly removed the supplies she needed from the cabinet and then sat on the bed to treat the wound. She applied a large blob of antibacterial cream to her hand and fingers and covered all of the surfaces of the wound with the cream. She then covered a swab with the cream and inserted it into the wound. The pain was nearly unbearable, but she had to do whatever she could to prevent an infection. The probing with the swab started the bleeding anew, but Shannon had anticipated this. She had a dressing sitting nearby with a blob of antibacterial cream already on it. She held this firmly in place over the wound and then used her chin to hold it in place while she used her left arm to wrap the dressing tightly with an elastic bandage. The pressure from the bandage quickly stopped the renewed bleeding.

Shannon eased herself down onto the bed and lay there sobbing. A flood of emotions swept through her body. Feelings of rage, anger, futility, guilt, and vengeance all surged through her body. More than anything, the need to avenge the deaths of her husband and son tore at her. Shannon looked at her right arm and knew it would be weeks, or months before it would be back to normal. Until then she would focus her energies on recovering. She'd need a week or so to recover from the blood loss she'd suffered. The tissue damage in her shoulder would likely heal on its own. She'd have to work hard to regain her strength and range of motion, but those were minor problems. First, she'd have to survive. She could only hope that her cabin was hidden from those hunting her as she was in no position now to offer serious resistance.

She had two portable police scanners operating in the cabin. One was tuned to the known police frequencies; the other was searching for any unknown frequency that was transmitting. Shannon was hoping that whoever was hunting her would use radios and that she could find the frequency. The police frequencies were abuzz with activity as dozens of police cars flooded the area. Shannon listened to the scanners until tiredness finally wore her down and she drifted off to sleep.

* * *

Roger Bentley took the call backstage at the convention. The convention center was buzzing with excitement. They were just minutes away from Eleanor taking the stage and making her announcement that she was being forced to drop from the race due to her health. The press was buzzing with anticipation thinking the big announcement would be the vice presidency. Hector was pacing the floor nearby.

"Did you find her?" asked Roger.

"Not yet, but we will soon," said Craig Burke. "We've got people looking every place she's likely to show up. We'll find her."

"Get it done," said Roger as he disconnected the phone. Hector came over to him.

"Did they find her?" asked Hector.

"Not yet. It's just a question of time. She's probably dead or dying someplace. She won't be a problem."

"We can't have this go public."

"Don't worry about it. We've got the situation covered."

The auditorium had now erupted into applause as Eleanor was announced and took the stage. Hector's pacing increased in tempo. There was a gasp from the audience as Eleanor broke the news of her diagnosis. Eleanor could be heard explaining the situation and then the audience broke into applause as Eleanor changed the tone to announce her choice for her replacement. In the back of the auditorium, party lackeys were unwrapping the new banners and placards and starting to distribute them through the crowd.

Eleanor brought the audience to their feet as she introduced Hector to the crowd. The curtains parted and Hector and his family strode out to take the stage. Eleanor embraced Hector and then stood aside as the spotlights trained on Hector.

CHAPTER FOUR

The search for Shannon had exasperated all of the parties involved. The only people who were more frustrated than the police were Craig Burke and his men. They had the advantage of knowing more about Shannon than the police, but that information was of no help as Shannon had effectively disappeared. After a week of futility, Craig returned to Washington for an uncomfortable meeting with his boss.

"What happened?" asked Roger Bentley.

"We got unlucky. We had everything set up. We were planning on using the safety of her husband and kid to get the videos. In a worst-case scenario, we'd just kill them all and torch everything. Their Hummer went further into the field than we'd anticipated. When the husband got out and came towards us we sent four men to the vehicle to get the girl and her kid.

"She saw what was going on and jumped into the driver's seat and tried to get between us and her husband to shield him. We opened fire on them. We killed him and the kid. Wounded her, but she spun the Hummer around and drove off into the nearby woods. We figured she'd get stuck in the woods, but the vehicle just plowed through to a dirt road. We ended up being about three minutes behind her by the time she reached the convenience store where she stole the truck.

"We lost another couple of minutes in getting to the second convenience store. After that, she's just disappeared. We can't find her. The locals can't find her. She's either dead or very well hidden."

"Let's hope she's dead," muttered Roger. "I can't imagine what kind of mood she's in."

"We can't live on hope here. As dangerous as she was before, she's probably ten times more dangerous now. We've taken everything she loves away from her. We can't drop this until we know she's dead."

"What about the video?"

"We didn't find it, or any leads pointing us to it. If it was in the house then it's gone. The house burned to the ground and I've got a couple of guys on the cleanup team who are looking for anything we might have missed or that escaped the flames but it looks like everything there is trash. We've got the hard drives from every computer they own and our forensics guys can find no trace of the videos or any hint of any place they may have been stashed. I'm thinking the video is gone. If she still had it she'd likely have released it by now if she thought Hector was behind this. Given the media attention he's getting, and their past issues, she's probably assumed he's behind this."

"What are you doing now?"

"We're still actively looking for her. We've got investigators checking every contact we can identify. We're looking at any medical facility where she could get treatment for her wounds. We've got teams in place monitoring the funeral of her family. We're checking everyone who attends. We've got people in place to monitor the graves and other places she might visit. Every bus line, taxi, train, and plane out of the area has been checked and they came back clean. She'll pop up somewhere. When she does, we'll be ready for her."

* * *

The week of rest had allowed Shannon's wound to heal. Her shoulder was still stiff and sore and was lacking in range of motion, but she could safely move without much pain or fear of bleeding. Her blood count was up to a good level. She was now capable of carrying out limited physical activity. Her right arm was still a bit limited, but she was functional once again.

The activity on the police scanners had died down to a normal level. Whoever was behind the ambush hadn't been using radios to communicate, or they were operating on a frequency her scanners couldn't find. Local news reports had pretty much dropped the story. Shannon did not doubt that the police and those who had attacked her were still actively hunting for her. Because of this, it was time to change her appearance. Among the supplies Shannon had stocked in the cabin was a selection of hair coloring and wigs. From now on, she would need multiple disguises for any public outing.

Shannon knew this area intimately. She was fairly sure she knew where anyone from outside the area would be staying. There were only two hotels in the immediate area. One was a major chain hotel with security cameras and all the amenities. Shannon was pretty sure that a higher-end hotel would not be used by those hunting her. They were most likely staying someplace where they would leave less of a trail. There was no place better for that than the Sea-Air Motel. The Sea-Air

Motel was a run-down motel that dated back to the fifties. It was essentially a long line of rooms stretching back from the road with a parking lot alongside the rooms. There were woods behind the motel and parking lot. If there were people here hunting her then that would be the most likely place to find them.

She dyed her light brown hair jet black. She then cut it very short, making it easier to quickly hide the hair under a wig or hat. Contact lenses changed her eyes from their normal blue to brown. Dark pants and a dark shirt replaced the sweats she'd worn since the attack. Heavy boots completed the outfit. Shannon waited until dark and then left her refuge. She carried a backpack filled with items she might need. The half-moon cast enough light for her to see. Shannon spent several hours walking through woods and fields to reach the woods that backed onto the motel. She positioned herself among the trees where she could watch the comings and goings. Six cars were parked in the parking lot. Shannon took mental note of the cars and then settled down to watch.

It was just after dawn when the first stirrings could be seen at the motel. Two men came out of one of the rooms and went across the street to the diner. The two men were well-built and moved in a way that immediately drew Shannon's attention. She watched when they came back a couple of minutes later carrying two bags of food and a tray of coffee. There were eight cups of coffee in the tray. Shannon watched as they reentered the motel room. She made note of the room.

After a half-hour, four men came out of that room and walked to one of the cars parked in the lot. One man stopped and looked back at the motel. He said something to the others and then walked over to an adjacent motel room and knocked loudly on the door. The door opened and a brief conversation ensued, then four more men came from that room and walked to the car alongside the one that the other three men were in. All eight men now got into the two cars and drove away. Shannon looked at her watch.

It was almost an hour later when one of the cars returned to the lot with four different men in it. Shannon watched as these four men got out and entered one of the rooms that the other men had left. A few minutes later a second car with four more men pulled in and those men went into the other room that had recently been vacated. Shannon smiled and slid back further into the woods to plot her next move.

She was ready when twelve hours later, the pattern repeated itself. The eight men who had come in this morning were now loading themselves into the cars. Shannon waited in the woods until the second car had pulled away. She then moved through the parking lot to reach the first motel room door. She listened at the door for several seconds, then hearing nothing she knocked on the door. No sound came from within the room. The locks on the doors at this motel were no deterrent for Shannon. Within seconds she had the lock opened and slid into the room, easing the door closed behind her.

It was obvious that housekeeping was skipping this room. Trash littered the floor. Empty coffee cups and beer bottles were strewn everywhere. In addition to the two beds, two cots had also been set up in the cramped space. On one wall was a series of photographs and computer-generated images of Shannon. Several of the photographs had been taken just before the attack. They showed Shannon playing with Tyler in their yard the day before the attack. Shannon fought hard to suppress her tears when she saw the photographs. The photographs showing Tyler and Jack all had "X" marks crossing them off, but Shannon's image was circled in red. A few of the photographs were computer generated to show what she might look like with different hair colors and styles. Shannon was dismayed to find that one of them was a pretty good match for her current appearance. A computer and printer were plugged into the wall. A digital camera was sitting nearby.

The men were planning on staying for a while. A small refrigerator had been brought into the room. Shannon opened it and found the men's stash of beer. The interior of the fridge was filled with beer. She looked about the room and found what she was looking for. There was an air conditioning duct facing the beds. Shannon removed the grille covering the duct and reached into her backpack and removed one of the small cameras she'd brought from the cabin. She slid the camera into the duct and then reinstalled the grille. She briefly opened her backpack and removed her laptop computer to verify that the camera showed what she needed to see. It did. She looked at her watch. She still had enough time to finish her tasks. The two rooms had a door connecting them and Shannon moved from one motel room to the other one. In here she repeated her camera planting and then retreated to the woods.

She'd only been in the woods a few minutes when the first of the returning cars showed up. Shannon turned on her computer and watched as the men came in. The four men shed their coats and then sprawled about the room. One of the men went to the refrigerator and soon all four were drinking bottles of beer. While they were doing this, the second car pulled into the lot. Those four men went to the adjoining room and followed the same pattern. Shannon watched as the men joked with each other for a bit. The door between the adjoining rooms was briefly opened and more beer was passed around.

After a couple of hours of sitting around, drinking beer, and watching television, the men started to settle down for some sleep before their next twelve-hour shift. Shannon had learned what she needed to know. She made her way back through the fields to her cabin. She would need some supplies before returning.

* * *

Hector had now spent several days on the campaign trail and the initial polling was very favorable. Eleanor had held a three-point lead in the polls leading up to the convention. Hector had now expanded that lead to nine points. A large part of that was due to the bump after the convention, but Hector had a good message that he was repeating endlessly and the public seemed to be behind him. The crowds were growing with each stop and unless something dramatic happened, it looked like a near certainty that he'd achieve his goal of winning the presidency.

He was getting a briefing on foreign policy when his top aide interrupted and told him that Roger Bentley would like to see him. Hector excused the briefer and greeted his father-in-law as he entered the room.

"Things are going very well," said Roger as he took the offered seat. "The polling is great and your numbers are still improving. If your numbers were only due to the post-convention bump they should be settling back, but you're still gaining ground."

"Keeping Eleanor's illness secret was a smart move," said Hector. "Our opponent was gearing his campaign to defeating Eleanor and now that she's out, his campaign is in shambles. We've got them on the run. The key is to keep them on the run. We can't have any gaffes."

"Just stick to the script and we should be okay. Everything's come together perfectly so far."

"Is there any word on Sara?"

"No," said Roger with a smile. "I'm thinking she's dead. She probably drove the car off the road when she died and it's in a river, or the woods someplace. If she was alive we would have found her. Every surveillance camera in the area has been checked and the car never left the area. We've still got people on the ground looking for her, but most likely she's dead and gone. We don't have to worry about her anymore. If she pops up, then we'll get rid of her, but I think she's gone."

* * *

The next evening found Shannon back in place in the woods behind the motel. In her backpack were the supplies she'd picked up at the cabin and nearby stores. She settled down and watched, waiting for the right moment to make her move.

At the same time as the previous evening, the eight men came out and drove off. Shannon quickly entered the motel room. She locked the door behind her and made her way to the refrigerator. She replaced the bottles of beer in the refrigerator with bottles that she had bought and altered. She'd finished and returned to the nearby woods when the first group of men had returned. Like before, they settled into their routine, and the beer was passed out. Shannon was pleased to see that each man was drinking. The second group joined them in a few more minutes and soon all eight men were drinking her tainted beer. Shannon turned off the computer to conserve its batteries. Experience had taught her that in an hour, the eight men would be semi-conscious at best. That would be when she'd make her move.

* * *

David Friedman and his partner Walter were running out of patience.
"Where the hell are they?" asked Walter.
"Damned if I know," said David. Their relief crew was now nearly thirty minutes late and they weren't answering their phones.
"What do we do?" asked Walter.
"We've given them every opportunity to respond," said David. "We'd better call this in. I hate to get them in trouble, but we can't stay out here forever. If something's gone wrong, then the sooner we get things moving, the better."
David called the emergency number and relayed his concerns to their coordinator. The call was evaluated as being serious enough to be forwarded to Craig Burke. Craig had stopped by the town to check up on the progress of the investigation and the call was relayed to his suite in the chain hotel in town. He listened and frowned at the news. He hung up the phone and then called his security detail. The group left the lobby of the hotel a few minutes later and made their way to the Sea-Air motel to determine what was going on.
The two vehicles were where they should be, but the men were not in sight. Craig and his security detail approached the motel room door and knocked loudly. No answer could be heard coming from inside.
"Take the door," said Craig to his beefiest guard. The guard leaned against the door and then shouldered it inwards. The five men entered the room with their guns drawn. There was no need for the guns as Shannon had long since left. All four of the men in the room were now naked and hog-tied. Their mouths were covered with duct tape and their throats had been slit. Blood stained the bedding and was pooling on the floor. Photos of the men now hung where the photos of Shannon and her family had been. Each man's photo had an 'X' through it, just as Shannon's husband's and son's photos had. The computer was gone as was the digital camera. All of the men's guns and wallets were also missing.
"Holy shit!" muttered one of the guards.
"Check the other room!" ordered Craig.

That room revealed the same scene. Craig walked through the carnage and marveled at what he saw. Eight highly trained, well-armed men had been taken down by a wounded woman. This wasn't going to be pretty.

"What do we do now?" asked one of his bodyguards who was looking a bit pale.

"Call our guys in the field," ordered Craig. "Warn them to be on their toes. She knows we're here. She's come out of hiding. If she wasn't armed before, she is now. We're officially at war gentlemen."

* * *

Sheriff Underwood had just gotten into his patrol car when his cell phone rang. He looked at the caller ID and didn't recognize the number.

"Hello," said the sheriff.

"Hi, Tommy," said Shannon. "I'll bet you weren't expecting to hear from me."

"Shannon? Where are you? Are you okay?"

"I'm alive. I'm sorry about the trouble I've caused you. I've got some information for you."

"Come on in. I can help you."

Shannon laughed before replying. "You have no idea how dangerous that would be. You can't protect me. The people who want me dead would go around, or through you to get to me. They'd endanger Celia and the kids to make you comply. You can't help me now. I know what I need to know and I know what I need to do. I'm just calling you now to give you a heads up on some information you should know."

"I can help you. I can see to it that they don't threaten you, Celia, or the kids."

"Tommy, these are really bad people who are after me. They have no respect for you, the law, or the lives of your wife and children. They will do whatever it takes to get me out of the picture. If you get in their way, they will remove you, one way or another. You have no idea what I'm up against. You don't know these people. I do. They've killed before and they'll kill again. The only way to stop them is by taking them out. There is no security you can provide that they can't bypass. These are people without conscience. They will do whatever they want to do. They've got friends in the highest of places."

"Shannon, we'll find you no matter what. I can explain the stolen cars, but you've got to come in."

"I can't Tommy," said Shannon wistfully. "Tell Celia and the kids I'm thinking about them and they'll be in my prayers. Now, do you want my information or not?"

"What do you have?"

"Eight of the men who were involved in killing Jack and Tyler are currently in rooms fifteen and sixteen of the Sea-Air Motel. Those eight men aren't going anyplace. They were driving two gray SUVs. There are another eight men currently out looking for me. They've got several locations staked out. They're watching the cemetery, what's left of my house, the hospital, and your house. Two-man teams at each location. You'll want to pick those guys up. They won't be easy to find though. You'll have to hunt for them and you'll want to be pretty careful doing so. They won't want to be found. There are probably more of them running around that I don't know about yet. You've got to be careful Tommy. Don't use your radios to talk about this stuff. They're monitoring your radio frequencies. Use your cell phone to make your calls and round up the troops. You're going to need help on this."

"Who are these people?"

"They're employees of a private security firm. Officially they do security work at Federal prisons and the like. Truth be told, they're more of a private army than a security force. I'm just starting to do my research, but I'm pretty sure I know where this is all going to lead me."

"Are you sure you're okay?"

"I'm functional," said Shannon. "I'm not as strong as I need to be though. I'm going to disappear for a while to pull myself back together. Tell Celia I miss her and tell the kids I was asking about them."

"How can I get in touch with you?"

"You can't," said Shannon as she disconnected the phone, removed the SIM card, and threw it into the woods.

* * *

Sheriff Underwood was near the Sea-Air motel at the end of the call and he pulled to a stop just outside the parking lot and looked into the lot. The two SUVs that Shannon had mentioned were parked in the lot exactly where she'd said they'd be. There were also two men stationed outside the doors to the rooms Shannon had indicated and Tommy didn't like the look of these men. He used his cell phone to call in some support, and then, to test Shannon's theory he picked up the radio and called in that he would be investigating a disturbance at the Sea-Air Motel.

As soon as the radio message went out, one of the men outside the door of the motel room held a hand to his ear and frowned. He said something to the other man and then turned and knocked on the door of the motel room.

"What is it?" asked Craig Burke.

"Sheriff's coming this way to investigate reports of a disturbance here," said the member of his security detail who was monitoring the scanner and guarding the door.

"Great," said Craig sarcastically. "That's just what I needed."

"What do we do when he shows up?"

"Call me, and I'll come out and deal with him. How much time do I have before he gets here?"

"I'd say no time at all," said Sheriff Underwood who was now standing just behind the guard.

"Sheriff," said Craig nodding for his security men to step aside. "I was just getting ready to call you." Craig looked past the door and saw more patrol cars pulling in. Several deputies were now trailing the sheriff carrying shotguns and several State Police cars were now pulling into the parking lot also. "It looks like you called in the cavalry."

"I was warned to expect trouble."

"Trouble you found, but not from us," said Craig stepping back to let the sheriff see the interior of the room.

"What the hell?" asked the sheriff at the sight of the bound bodies and the pooling blood.

"She beat me here. These men are employees of mine who were assisting in the search for your Shannon Brewer. She found them before we could find her. When my men didn't report in this morning I came here to see what was wrong. What you see is pretty much what I found."

"Shannon did this?" asked Sheriff Underwood.

"Most likely. I won't know for sure until we lift some prints, but it fits her profile. The girl's good. I'll give her that."

"Okay," said the sheriff suddenly aware of the need for someone to be in charge. "I want everyone out of the room. Don't touch anything. I'll need statements from everyone here. Let's get these rooms secured and call in the detectives to handle the scene."

"You heard the man," said Craig Burke to his men. "Everyone out."

The sheriff looked down as Craig Burke walked past him and commented, "Nice boots."

"They're the standard issue for our guys."

"They're Boar boots aren't they?"

"Sure are. They're damned expensive too. They're worth it though. They're lightweight, durable, and give you good footing. I can get you a pair at cost if you'd like. We buy the damned things by the thousands so we get a pretty good price."

"I hadn't seen them around here before. I don't think anyone local sells them."

"They're kind of a specialty item. You most often find them in the military, or law enforcement fields. They're kind of pricey for hunters. Why are you so interested in my boots?"

"I got a report from the FBI this morning on the boot imprints we lifted from the site of Jack Brewer's murder," said Sheriff Underwood. "It said every impression except those by Jack Brewer were from Boar boots. That's quite a coincidence."

"I'm not trying to tell you how to do your business sheriff," said Craig testily. "But you've got the bodies of eight good men in these rooms behind you. I'd suggest you focus your energy on finding the person responsible for those murders and forget your shoe fetish."

"I know where my energies need to be focused," said Sheriff Underwood. "It'll be hours before this scene is processed. It might not even be until tomorrow with the number of bodies we've got here. I can't do anything on this investigation until I get those reports. I have the reports on the murders of Jack and Tyler Brewer. I know the boots that were worn by those who ambushed them. I have tire impressions from the vehicles that were used in the attack. I know the type of weapons that were used. Call me crazy, but I have a feeling you and your men were involved in those killings."

"Sheriff," said Craig with rising indignation. "You have no evidence implicating me or my men in any such activity. We were interested in finding Shannon Brewer, but we're not the only ones. Do you know how many people she's killed?"

"As far as I know, none," said Sheriff Underwood.

"We've now confirmed over fifty kills. That's not including these men here. The girl is a menace to society and she needs to be caught and held accountable."

"I'd have to see that information before I'd believe it."

"I'll provide it to you as soon as I get back to my hotel room. I've got the files back there. It'll be something of an eye-opener for you."

"I need you to call in the rest of your men," said the sheriff.

"What men?" asked Craig.

"The ones watching my house, the cemetery, the remains of the Brewer's house, and the hospital, plus any others you might have hanging around that I don't know about yet."

"Why are you here Sheriff?" asked Craig suspiciously. "She called you, didn't she? Son of a bitch! She called you!"

"Your men in the field," reminded the sheriff, confirming the accusation without saying a word. "I'm sending cars to those locations. I want them to walk out with their hands up and surrender to my men. You will call them and advise them of that. If they refuse to comply, then we will hunt them down. I've got canine teams on the way if they don't come out voluntarily. And you will not replace those men. Is that clear?"

"What did she say?" demanded Craig. "When did you talk to her? Goddamn it! You can't help protect this woman! You have no idea how dangerous she is!"

"I'm just doing my best to enforce the laws of this state. Are you willing to call your men and have them surrender, or do I have to use the dogs to flush them out?"

"Give me a phone," muttered Craig.

* * *

Shannon had watched from the woods as Sheriff Underwood and his men raided the motel. Once she was sure there was to be no violence in the raid, she abandoned her position and made her way back to her cabin. Come nightfall, she would leave the area, never to return. Until then, she gathered up the supplies she would need.

* * *

Sheriff Underwood had never seen the sheriff's offices so crowded. Every room now held an officer and one or more of those pulled in from the security firm. Each man from the firm had now been questioned and their stories were remarkably similar. So similar in fact, that it was apparent that they were operating off a memorized script. Sheriff Underwood was now sitting at his desk with Craig Burke sitting opposite him. Craig Burke's hotel room had been searched and the files from the room were now sitting in front of Sheriff Underwood.

"Pretty impressive," said Sheriff Underwood perusing the files still not sure he believed any of what he was reading.

"That woman is a cold-blooded killer," said Craig.

"I notice there isn't any mention of who she killed in the last five years. Did she kill anyone during that span?"

"Not that we know of."

"Then why are you hunting her now?"

"What do you mean? She's a professional killer. She should be taken off the streets."

"Your records show that this hunt started recently," said the sheriff closing yet another file. "Why are you hunting her now? Who's behind this investigation?"

"I'm not telling you that. It's obvious you have some feelings for this woman and are trying to help her. I don't need her getting any more help than she already has."

"I'm guessing that she was the target when you and your men killed Jack and Tyler."

"We didn't kill Jack and Tyler Brewer," restated Craig for the hundredth time.

"I'm not so sure of that."

"Sheriff, you may not believe this, but we're the good guys here. Shannon Brewer used to be called Sara X and she was a cold-blooded killer. Just look what she did to my men who were looking for her."

"The Shannon Brewer I knew was not a killer. I don't know what she did before she came here, but she was as solid a citizen as I've ever been around during her time here. These files you have are worthless. I've checked on a few of them and in every case, the official cause of death was, and still is listed as natural causes. As far as I can tell, this is all fabricated. You can't argue murder when in nearly every case the person is listed as dying by natural causes. As to these so-called connections, isn't everyone in Hollywood supposedly connected to Kevin Bacon in some way? I suspect if you looked at suspicious deaths anywhere you'd find similar connections."

"She kills people and makes them look like death by natural causes. It's what she does. There are also the gun and knife murders where she left fingerprints behind. How do you explain those?"

"I don't have Shannon's fingerprints to compare to those that were collected," reminded the sheriff. "She's never been arrested and her prints aren't on file. We've got prints from the cars she drove that match up, but I can't say for certain that those are her prints. With her home and other buildings now destroyed along with all of her possessions I'll likely never get her fingerprints unless she turns up again sometime, and given what you guys have done to her and her family, I don't expect her to turn up anytime soon.

"Also in regards to the earlier fingerprints, in nearly all of those cases the eyewitness descriptions of the suspects don't come close to matching that of Shannon. What's going on here? Why do you want her dead? Why are you willing to kill her husband and child to get to her?"

"Sheriff, I'm telling you for the final time. We didn't kill her husband and child. As far as I know, she may have done it herself. We're just trying to find her and get her off the streets before she kills again."

"The person you're looking for isn't Shannon Brewer. I know her. This isn't her. She's not a killer."

"I've talked to some of the people who have hired her and I know what they've told me," said Craig Burke. "This woman is a cold-blooded killer."

"Who are these people you've talked to?" asked the sheriff. "I don't see any names mentioned in the files. Or is one or more of them your client?"

Before Craig could answer Sheriff Underwood's secretary knocked on his office door and handed Tommy Underwood a message.

"What the hell?" said Tommy after reading the message. "The Governor is calling me?"

"I've checked it out," said the secretary. "It's him."

"Okay," said the sheriff nodding to his secretary. "Line two?" His secretary nodded and then stepped out of the room closing the door behind her. He picked up the phone and pressed the button for line two.

"Sheriff Underwood," he said into the phone.

"Sheriff, this is Governor Small. I understand you're detaining some employees of the Bentley Security Agency."

"That's correct," said Sheriff Underwood wondering how the governor had heard of this.

"I'd like you to release those men," said the Governor. "I can personally vouch for them."

"I can't do that sir. These men were found with eight murdered men. They may very well be responsible for the murder of two of our local citizens. I'm awaiting the results of tests that we've sent out to the state police lab for verification on some boot and tire impressions that were found at the murder scene. Eight additional employees of that firm were found staking out various locations in the area, including my home. I'm not releasing anyone until I know exactly what is going on."

"Sheriff," continued Governor Billy Small. "I can assure you that these men are of high character and are above suspicion. They are not your problem. You should be focusing your energy on finding the woman behind all of this."

"Begging your pardon sir, but Jack Brewer was a friend of mine. I was Tyler Brewer's godparent. Jack and Shannon Brewer were godparents to my son and daughter. I'm being fed a bunch of bull that makes no sense. I believe that at least some of these men are responsible for the deaths of Jack and Tyler Brewer. I'm not releasing anyone until I have to. I've now got a bunch of people here who are reciting the same story. They are so identical in their stories that it's obvious that they are working off a script."

"Maybe their identical stories are because they are all telling you the truth," said the Governor. "I'm afraid you're letting your interest in this investigation taint your objectivity. These men are not the enemy." The Governor paused for a few seconds before continuing. "What are your plans for the future?"

"What do you mean?" asked Sheriff Underwood.

"Sheriff is an elected office. I can pretty much assure you that you'll have the full support of the party for as long as you want the job as long as you proceed responsibly in this investigation."

"I am proceeding responsibly in this investigation."

"Not if you continue to hold these men. I can guarantee you that the report from the state police will vindicate these men. They are not responsible for the deaths of Jack and Tyler Brewer. The longer you detain them, the further away the true perpetrator can get. You've got to let these people go. If you fail to do so, then perhaps the party will have to look at other options for your position as Sheriff."

"Sir, are you threatening me?"

"I would consider it good advice rather than a threat. The men you are holding are not the ones you should be looking for. They have nothing to do with this investigation and should be freed immediately. I can assure you that your party will be very appreciative should you reach the same conclusion and release these men. Funding for your department and staffing is largely controlled by our party. If you show that you are not supportive of the party, then perhaps the party shouldn't be supportive of you. Do you understand me?"

"Yes, Sir," said Tommy coldly. "Thank you for calling."

Tommy Underwood hung up the phone and stared long and hard at Craig Burke.

"Who the hell are you? And what are you hiding?"

"I'm not hiding anything," said Craig Burke.

The secretary knocked on the door again and stuck her head in.

"What is it?"

"Senator Billings wants to talk to you," said the secretary.

"What the hell is going on here?" asked Tommy as he picked up the phone.

* * *

Craig Burke made the call he dreaded as he was being driven from the Sheriff's office after his release.

"I called to let you know that I've been released."

"It took long enough," said Roger Bentley.

"The sheriff wasn't very impressed by the pressure placed upon him. He almost seemed more determined to hold me with each call. It was only when he got the negative report from the state police lab that he finally relented. We're going to have to keep an eye on him."

"He's out of office at the next election. He won't even win the primary. If he wants to buck the party, then he'll see the price he has to pay. Where's the girl?"

"I don't know. Our best chance to track her down is now probably gone. I was going to bring in a dog team to track her from the motel, but it's been raining for the last hour and whatever scent trail she left is probably gone. I'll still put a team in the woods and see if they can track her, but it won't be easy."

"Did she kill eight of our men?"

"Yes. It looks like she drugged them and then killed them. It was crude but effective. She was sending us a message. The sheriff sent the beer to the state police lab to be tested. It should be interesting to see what turns up."

"Think he'll share the report?"

"No chance," said Craig.

"That's okay. We can get it directly from the lab. Our guys there handled the shoe and tire impressions well, so they won't mind forwarding that report to us."

* * *

Hector Esteban took the call from Roger Craig and listened as the events that took place in the motel room were explained to him.

"So, she's still alive then?" said Hector.

"It looks that way. This could have been unrelated, but it looks like it came directly from her."

"We can't have that video come out during the campaign."

"Don't worry about it. She's killed her credibility by killing my men. We've got a nationwide all points bulletin out for her now. We'll find her pretty soon and put this threat behind us. It was just my guys looking for her, but now every law enforcement officer in the country is looking for her after this. She can't run or hide for long. When she sticks her head up, we'll cut it off."

* * *

Sheriff Underwood called in one of his deputies.

"What is it boss?" asked Pete Henderson.

"Did you document those boot and tire impressions?"

"Sure did. I've got digital images of the top, bottom, front, and back, of each boot. We even set the boots atop the photocopier and printed out the sole pattern. I've got images of each section of tire tread also. Why?"

"Did you share them with the State Troopers who were picking up the stuff?"

"There was no need to. They had the originals so why would they need the prints?"

"I want copies of all of those images."

"What's going on?"

Sheriff Underwood paused for a few seconds before continuing. "What do you know about the State Police lab?"

"They're pretty good at what they do. I've only been there a couple of times, but it was fairly impressive."

"How long do you think it would take them to give us an analysis on the boot and tire prints?"

"Analyzing twenty plus pairs of boots and twelve tire impressions? I would guess maybe two or three days if they weren't doing anything else. If they're backed up it might take a few weeks. Why?"

"They sent me a full report an hour ago saying that there were no matches," said Sheriff Underwood sliding the faxed report across his desk.

The deputy read the report and frowned.

"I don't understand this. They just left here a few hours ago. They shouldn't even have this stuff logged into the system yet, let alone have a full analysis performed. Just the paperwork required for transferring evidence should take longer than that. There's no way this can be true."

"That's what I thought. I called the lab and the director confirmed the information you see in that report. He insists that there are absolutely no matches and that they were very thorough."

"What the hell is going on here?" asked the deputy.

"I don't know, but I don't like it. I want copies of those images. I'm going to see if I can get the FBI lab to take a look at the images and see what they say."

"They'll want the original boots and tires. And the state police lab now has them."

"Want to bet they'll give them back to us?"

"I'm guessing no," said the deputy.

"They'll claim there was no match, therefore there is no evidentiary value. They'll notify the rightful owners to come and reclaim the items. Chances are they've already been released. We might have missed our best chance to nail these bastards."

"If we can't trust the State Police lab, then who can we trust?"

"I'm not sure we can trust anyone," said Sheriff Underwood tilting back in his chair. "I've got to think about this for a while."

* * *

Shannon was pleased to finally leave the immediate area. She was heading west. She had an old client out west that had let her crash in a cabin on his property in the past and she was heading that way again. She now had to be more careful than she'd ever been before. She needed time to rebuild her strength. She needed time to think through her next move. She now knew who the enemy was. It was now simply a question of how to punish them. Death, while emotionally satisfying was too easy a way out for those who had destroyed her life.

CHAPTER FIVE

Sheriff Tommy Underwood wasn't surprised to find his wife still up and waiting for him even though he was about six hours late in finally getting home. He was even less surprised to find that she'd fixed him some fresh supper. As he sat down for the meal Celia sat beside him and wrapped her arms around him.

"So, hard day?" asked Celia with a smile, already knowing the answer.

"I'm getting too old for this job," said Tommy Underwood enjoying the warm embrace of his wife as she kept her arms wrapped around him.

"You made the news again," said Celia knowing that appearing in front of the press was the one thing her husband hated the most about his job. "You looked good. You're getting a lot of air time."

"Not by choice."

"Is it true what they said?"

"What's that?" asked Tommy as he sat at the table.

"That those men were after Shannon?"

"It looks that way."

"Who were they?"

"They were an assortment of types. Some of them are ex-cons, mostly ex-military types. A couple of them are foreigners. It's an interesting mix. Turns out they all work for the same security firm, Bentley Security."

"I've never heard of them."

"They provide guards for prisons, hotels, resorts and offer private security to people, or groups who are willing to pay enough. One of their guys was talking to one of my deputies. He explained that they sort through the prison population and hire the best of the ex-cons as soon as they come out. The same is true for the military. They sort through those coming out and skim off the cream of the crop. The guy tried to recruit him."

"I hope he told them where to go."

Tommy put down the fork he'd just picked up and looked at his wife. He decided he had to ask her the question that had been nagging him all day.

"Did she call you?"

"Who?"

"Shannon. Did she call you today?"

"No. I haven't talked to her since before this all started. Why?"

"She called me."

"Oh my God!" exclaimed Celia. "How was she? Was she okay? Where is she? What did she say?"

"This is starting to sound like the press conference. How about we deal with one question at a time?"

"I'm sorry. It's just that I've been so worried about her."

"I don't think we have to worry about her too much. She sounded a bit tired but otherwise okay. It looks like she killed those eight men in the motel. We haven't gotten all of the reports back yet, but the indications are that she killed them."

"Were they the ones who killed Jack and Tyler?"

"I think so."

"Then that's good! They should die for what they did!"

"Getting to be a bit of a vigilante, are you? What about fair trials and all of that?"

"How many bad guys have you seen get off on technicalities?" asked Celia. "If she knows they did it, then more power to her for getting rid of them. I'd do the same thing if I could. Was that all of them?"

"I don't think so. We found more of their guys at the motel. Shannon told me where to find eight more. We brought them all into the offices and spent most of the day trying to get answers out of them. They weren't overly cooperative. I had to release the lot of them even though I'm pretty sure at least some of them were involved in this whole thing."

"Why did you release them?"

"There was a lack of evidence. What evidence we'd collected was dismissed by the state police lab. It looks like they're all going to walk away from this unscathed."

"Unless Shannon catches up to the rest of them and takes them out."

"I'm kind of hoping she does," admitted Tommy. "Do you know they had two men watching our house?"

"What?" asked a now visibly angry Celia. "Some of the people who murdered Jack and Tyler were watching our house?"

"Yes. They were on the hill across the road keeping an eye on us. Supposedly they were trying to see if we were sheltering Shannon. I wouldn't be surprised to find they were also eavesdropping on us. They might still be. They were watching everyone who might have contact with Shannon hoping to catch her. I'm going to be keeping a closer watch on things around here for a while. It looks like they're leaving town, but I don't trust them."

Celia was now pacing the floor. Tommy could see that she was troubled and wished he hadn't shared that last piece of information with her.

"I'm sorry. I shouldn't have told you that."

"It just creeps me out knowing that murderers have been watching me and the kids. I saw what they did to Tyler. I know what they did to Jack. If they try to come within a mile of my kids, I'll kill them! If you find them in town again, tell them that!"

"I don't want you doing anything. The deputies and I know what to look for now. We're going to do our best to keep them out of town. If they insist on coming in, then we're going to make their lives miserable. You leave that to us. These are bad people who have a lot of political cover. They seem to be able to do whatever they want without consequence."

"What do you mean?"

"The report from the state police lab that exonerated them was faxed to me less than two hours after the items left my office. The lab's a half-hour away. The normal procedure for handling evidence should have taken a couple of hours just to log everything in. This kind of evidence should have taken hours, or days to examine and analyze, yet I had a final report on my desk in less than two hours. I also got a call from the Governor vouching for the men, along with another call from Senator Billings also vouching for the men. There were also calls from local politicians vouching for these guys. It was made abundantly clear to me that any future I have in elected office depends on my releasing these men and not pursuing the investigation in their direction."

Celia stared at her husband for a few long seconds before replying.

"I hope you told them all to go fuck themselves!" muttered Celia viciously.

"No," said Tommy. He fought hard to suppress a smile at hearing the "F" word coming from his wife's lips. Celia rarely cursed and never used the "F" word. He had expected such a reaction from her and was not disappointed. "Shannon warned me about them. She warned me that they'd come after you guys if I didn't cooperate with them. I'm thinking she was correct. I released the suspects. I'm going to be keeping an eye on things, but if I can't pursue the investigation without endangering you and the kids, I'm not sure I want to take that risk."

"Like hell! You will find the people responsible for the deaths of Tyler and Jack and you will arrest them! Don't worry about me and the kids. I'll deal with anyone who comes after us! If they think Shannon is dangerous, they haven't seen anything! Let them come!"

"It's not that simple. They can see to it that I don't get a chance for another shot at the office of sheriff. They can control our future."

"Do you want to be a paper cutout of a sheriff who answers to politicians, or do you want to do what you swore to do when you took this job? The man I married would not back down from these thugs! Let them come after me! Let them touch one hair on my kids' head and they'll see what an angry woman is! You do your job, or so help me God I'll do it for you! I am not having these murderers running around unchecked!"

"You're sure of this?" asked Tommy already knowing the answer.

"Do you have to ask? Now, what are you going to do?"

"I've already done it. I've sent copies of the imprints to the FBI lab for analysis. I have another copy going to a guy I know in Jersey who does this kind of work freelance. Once I know for sure that these guys are behind those murders then we'll move forward. But you have to understand I can only find them and arrest them. Prosecution with that kind of political pressure might be a problem. Our prosecutor is a political animal. Even if he brings charges there might be only a minimal effort on his part. Chances are these guys will walk anyway."

"You do your job. If the prosecutor drops the ball, then I'll deal with him. He thinks these people have political power, he'll see where true political power lies. If he doesn't do his job I'll personally see to it that he never gets elected again."

"How would you do that?" asked Tommy warily.

"You're forgetting that I went to school with our prosecutor. I know more things about him than he'd like to think about. Trust me. If he crosses us on this then his future in politics is gone. I can put more political pressure on him than you'd believe. I can tell the world who our prosecutor is and there's no way he can spin himself out of the truth. Let me worry about him."

"I knew there was a reason I married you."

"Why did they kill Jack and Tyler?"

"I don't think either of them was the target. It sounds like they were trying to get to Shannon and the other two just got caught up in it. According to the files these guys had on Shannon she had quite an interesting past."

"What do you mean by interesting?"

"The files indicate that Shannon was a contract killer. I'm guessing she'd done some work for these guys, or someone close to them, and they were afraid she might talk so they were trying to silence her."

"Shannon was a contract killer? Our Shannon?"

"It looks that way."

"Do you think Shannon did all of those things?"

"The files are in my briefcase. I'm not sure how much of it I believe, but on paper, it looks like it was her."

The phone rang and the sheriff excused himself. He came back a few seconds later and told Celia that he was going to have to go back out for a few minutes. He had to tell her twice as Celia had removed the files from his briefcase and was busily perusing them and not paying any attention to him.

* * *

Craig Burke was fairly certain that Shannon had called the sheriff to notify him of her handiwork, so he had one of the hacker teams at Bentley go to work to try and determine if she had, and how many times she'd called him. Their report was now on his desk and it showed that she'd only called him once and that the call had lasted for three minutes. They were then able to trace Shannon's phone back to the store where she'd bought it and every place where she'd used it.

Craig hadn't been surprised to find that the call to the sheriff originated from the woods adjacent to the motel where his men had been killed. He studied the satellite images of the area and realized that he'd been within a hundred yards of her when she'd made the call. He sent two teams back to town. One team was to try and pick up Shannon's trail through the woods and another was sent to check out a second location where the phone had been activated.

The attempt to track Shannon through the woods met with immediate failure when deputies met the Bentley security search team as they entered the town and followed them wherever they went. The second team managed to get past the deputies to the cabin where Shannon had been hiding. They found it pretty much emptied. There were blood-stained bandages in the trash and some leftover freeze-dried meals, but the cabin was otherwise empty. Shannon had moved on. While they were examining the tire tracks leading into the nearby lake the sheriff drove up followed by three more patrol cars.

"This is private property gentlemen," said the sheriff. "I trust you've gotten written permission from the owner of this land to trespass upon it?"

"Do you have any idea who that owner would be?" asked the man heading the team.

"If you don't know, then I'm not about to tell you."

"The owner of this land is officially listed as being a dummy corporation. We have reason to believe it was set up by Shannon Brewer to hide her purchase of this land. We also have reason to believe that she was hiding here until recently."

"And why would you suspect that?"

"The cellular phone that she's been using was activated from that cabin over there. These tire tracks that run into the lake probably belong to the car that was stolen that she used for her getaway. I suspect you'll find the guns she stole also in the lake. There are blood-stained bandages in the trash behind the cabin. The cabin has been cleaned out now and she's gone, but from this location, she could reach just about any part of town she wanted to by moving through the woods without fear of detection."

"I'm going to have to ask you gentlemen to leave the area," said Sheriff Underwood. "I'll have to look into these allegations, for now, though I'll ask you, gentlemen, to get into your vehicle and follow my deputies back to my office where you'll provide statements to them."

One sheriff's car led the way back to the office while two more sheriff's department cars trailed along behind. Tommy and another deputy checked out the cabin.

"I didn't know this place was even here," muttered the deputy.

"Old man Higgins used to own this place," said the sheriff. "I'd pretty much forgotten about it. It used to be pretty run down, but it looks like someone took some time and money to fix it up a bit."

"Shannon Brewer?"

"It could be. I don't know for now. We'll have to look into the property records. We'll have to get a dive team out here to check the lake. We'll also need the detectives to come to the cabin to check for prints and any other evidence left behind."

The statements from the men from Bentley Security were brief and then the men were escorted out of town. Tommy Underwood had few doubts that this was far from over, but he and his men knew what to look for now and by God, these men would not operate freely in any area under his control, to hell with the consequences. Tommy returned home to find Celia sitting on the floor surrounded by the folders he'd brought home and furiously taking notes.

"Still at it?" asked Tommy.

"This is amazing," replied Celia. "I can't believe that the Shannon I knew did all of this."

"Well. I'm not sure how much of it she did. I called about a couple of the cases and found they were not treated as homicides, but natural deaths. Only a few of the cases were even considered suspicious from what I've gathered. The guys from Bentley seem to be pinning every suspicious death of anyone in any way linked to Shannon on her and I suspect they're overestimating her actions."

"I see you sent in some prints you thought were Shannon's."

"I wanted to confirm the information they'd given me."

"I was more impressed by what they didn't give you."

"What do you mean?"

"They gave you information about nearly every crime where her prints were found, but they omitted one case," said Celia holding up a paper. "They didn't give you the report from Los Angeles where she supposedly murdered four men. I called the LAPD and got a copy of the report from that incident faxed here. She reportedly killed four local thugs out there for some reason. She disappeared after that. They interviewed a guy named Kevin Seales who was dating her and who witnesses placed with her that night, but who claimed to know nothing. He claimed he left her after dinner and went home. The weird thing is there was a lot more of his interview that was blacked out. Why do you suppose they didn't give you this report?"

"They may have overlooked it."

"Or they could be trying to hide something. They sure didn't overlook anything else. How would you feel about me heading to California to chat up the guy she was dating back then?"

"Do you think you could find him?"

Celia glared back at Tommy before replying sarcastically, "What do you think?"

"Do you think you can get him to talk?" asked Tommy quickly changing the subject.

"I think so. I have a bunch of photos of Shannon and me together. If that's the same girl, he should consider me trustworthy and open up a bit. If he kept quiet to protect her, then he should be willing to talk to protect her now."

"Are you sure you want to do this?"

"What can it hurt? It'll get me out to Southern California for a while. I'll get some sun and see some sights and come back refreshed and recharged. Maybe I'll even get some answers as to what's going on."

"What about the kids?" asked Tommy.

"Mom will watch them while I'm gone. Given the fact that people have been watching our house, it might be a good idea to get them out of town for a while. I should be able to learn what I need in a day or two and then I'll be back. Mom will guard the kids like a pit bull. You don't have to worry about them while she's watching them."

"This can't be done officially. You'll have to be working this privately."

"That's not a problem. We have enough cash set aside to cover the costs without a problem. I'm just curious about what went down out there and this guy is our best bet to find out."

The investigation into the lake and cabin revealed exactly what the people from Bentley had suspected. The stolen car and the guns and wallets taken from the men in the motel room were all found in the lake. Fingerprints found in both the car and cabin matched those of Shannon Brewer. The blood-stained bandages were collected and sent out for DNA analysis.

* * *

Kevin Seales was surprised to find a woman waiting for him outside his office when he showed up to open it. He was somewhat confused by her appearance. She was dressed differently than most women around Los Angeles. Her clothes were tasteful but more modest and somewhat sturdier than what one typically saw on the streets of LA.

"I'm sorry to keep you waiting," said Kevin as he unlocked the door. He slid his hand in and flicked on the light switches and then held the door open for the woman. Kevin followed her into the office and took a seat behind his desk.

"It's my fault," said Celia Underwood sitting in the chair opposite the desk. "I'm afraid I'm still on east coast time."

"You're from the east?" asked Kevin as he turned on his computer and monitor.

"Virginia. A small town there you've probably never heard of."

"What brings you out here?"

"I've come to talk to you. I believe we have a mutual friend, Shannon Brewer?"

"I don't think I know a Shannon Brewer..." mused Kevin Seals.

"I'm sorry. You knew her as Sara Miller. The lack of sleep is making me a bit goofy this morning." She noticed the color flush from Kevin's face at the mention of Sara's name. Celia reached into her bag and pulled out some photographs and handed one to Kevin who was sitting and staring with a lost look on his face. "That's her isn't it?"

Kevin took the proffered photograph and looked at it for several seconds without really seeing it.

"Is that her?" prompted Celia once again.

Kevin shook himself from his stupor and looked at the photograph. It showed two women with their babies. One was the woman opposite him and the other was the woman he had known earlier. He handed the photograph back and nodded before replying.

"Yes. That's her. At least I think it is. Who are you?"

"I'm Celia Underwood. Shannon, I'm sorry, Sara is a good friend of mine and I'm afraid she's in some trouble and needs help."

"I don't doubt that she's in trouble, but I don't know what I can do to help. I only knew her for a short while and not all that well even then. Is she married now? Is that her kid?"

"She was," said Celia sadly. "Unfortunately her husband and son were murdered recently. Shannon was wounded but escaped. Has she contacted you?"

"No!" said Kevin wisely withholding the "Thank God!" that flashed through his mind. "Who are you again?"

"I'm just her friend and I want to find her. I want to help her. I want to find out who's trying to kill her. I'm hoping you can help me."

"I can honestly tell you that I haven't seen her, or talked to her in years. I'm not sure I want to get involved in anything involving her. Did she tell you about me?"

"No. Everything from her past was a mystery to me. I only learned about you from the police report that was taken after she reportedly killed those men out here."

Celia had noticed Kevin's eyebrows go up at the mention of the police report and she offered an explanation.

"My husband is the sheriff back home and that's how I saw the police report. He ran Shannon's fingerprints and they came up as matching those from a couple of crime scenes out here. We got the reports from those investigations and your interview was in there. I was intrigued by it and thought I'd come out and see what you remembered of that time. Much of your interview seemed to be blacked out. What do you remember of that time?"

"I remember too much. I wish I could forget some of it. I don't think you have to worry about helping that girl out. She's pretty good at taking care of herself."

"Believe me. I know she's capable of taking care of herself. I believe she killed eight of the men who killed her husband and son. I suspect she's hunting down the rest of them now. I'm hoping to find out who's behind this and I think you might know."

"She has a lot of enemies."

"Can you tell me what happened the last time you saw her?"

Kevin paused for a few seconds before replying. "We were out on a date. She said some people were following us. I thought she was playing some sort of game. She had me drive down an alley and then she hopped out and instructed me to drive to the end of the alley. I thought she was nuts, but I did what she said.

"A few seconds later a truck with its headlights off pulled into the alley and stopped behind my car. Four guys got out and started to move towards the car. Two of them had guns and one of the others had a bat and the other guy a pry bar. Sara came up behind one of the guys with a gun and quickly disarmed him and warned the others to drop their weapons. The other guy with the gun tried to get off a shot, but she killed him. The other two then dropped their weapons.

"We tied them up and loaded them and the dead guy into the back of the truck and then Sara drove the truck out into the country as I followed along behind her. She tortured the living guys to find out who had sent them and then killed them.

She then took me back to my apartment and that's the last I remember. She drugged me and left me there. I woke up the next morning asleep on the floor of the apartment. She left me a note apologizing for causing me trouble and wishing me well.

"About a week later a couple of detectives showed up at the place where I was working. They took me back to their offices for questioning about her. Somehow they'd connected her to the killings. They'd found a neighbor who identified me as being involved with her. I started to tell them everything I knew and then a superior who was monitoring everything came in and dismissed those guys. He advised me to forget everything and go back to my normal life. He made it kind of clear that I wasn't supposed to talk to anyone about what I'd heard or knew. He blacked out the notes the other detectives had taken and he then wrote what you saw. He told me to sign it. I did. He told me to forget about it all."

"Why would he tell you that?"

"She had a guy looking out for me to try and keep me out of trouble. This was the guy who had sent the thugs after her. She'd somehow changed his mind from wanting her dead to protecting me."

"Who was it?"

"You don't want to know."

"I have to know. They're hunting down my friend. I need to know who this guy was."

Kevin looked at her for several seconds before replying.

"They'll kill you if they know you know about them. They'll kill you, your husband, and your children. These people don't care. They're above the law. At least, they think they are."

"Who are they?"

"Do you know what Sara did for a living before she moved out here?"

"I've read some things, but I don't know how much I believe."

"What have you read?"

"I've read that she was a contract killer."

"She was a contract killer," agreed Kevin. "She killed for money. She told me so herself. She cleanly killed people so that their deaths looked natural. She said that she'd only kill someone who was going to be killed anyway. I guess that was her way of justifying the whole thing. By the time I met her she had more or less retired, or so she'd thought. Turned out one of those she'd done work for was worried about what she knew and what she might be able to prove. It was one of those former clients that tried to have her killed while I was with her. It was that same client of hers who got the police to forget about the case."

"Who was it?"

"I can't tell you that. Suffice to say this guy has enough power to get just about anyone eliminated, or deal with any threat. As far as I can tell, the only reason I'm still alive is that she threatened to kill him if anything happened to me and he's scared enough of her to let me live. If something should happen to her, then they might come after me."

"All the more reason to help me," said Celia. "If you give me a name I might be able to help keep Shannon alive and as long as she's alive, the threat of her helps keep you alive."

"I'd agree with that. But, I don't think they're overly worried about me anymore. They were keeping tabs on me for a while, but things have quieted down the last couple of years. I'd just as soon things stay quiet."

Celia removed another photograph: this one showing, Shannon, her husband, and Tyler, all smiling up at Celia's camera as she took their photograph just a few weeks earlier.

"They killed her husband and son. Do you think things are going to stay quiet? I can help, but I need a name. I need to know who's behind this."

Kevin stared long and hard at the photograph before replying.

"She'd killed his wife for him a few years earlier. He was talking with me in the gym and I showed him a photograph of Sara. He thought we were teaming up to blackmail him. He hired those men she killed to kill us both. He was scared to death of her. He thought she could destroy him."

"Who?"

"Hector Esteban," muttered Kevin quietly.

"Jesus!" muttered Celia. "Really?"

Kevin just nodded his head.

"Shannon killed his wife?"

"That's what she said. She did it in such a way as to make it look like a natural death. He was running for Senate then and the race was fairly tight. You can imagine what even that allegation would have done to his chances. He couldn't take that risk."

"How did you know him?"

"We went to the same gym," explained Kevin. "He was asking me if I was married and I said that I wasn't but that I was dating this hot new girl. I showed him her photo on my phone and he got kind of curt and left. That's when all hell broke loose. They followed me to her and then tried to kill us both. She saved my life. She probably still is saving my life. You've got to be very careful. These people have no respect for human life. They'll kill you and everyone around you if they think it might help them."

"I thought he was one of the good guys...."

"This just in," said Kevin dryly. "There are no good guys in politics. Some will draw the line at what they'll do to win, but they don't win so they disappear pretty quickly. Those who move up to seats of prominence do so by crushing everyone who gets in their way using any and every tool at their disposal. These are very bad boys. If they know that you know, they will crush you."

"Why do you keep quiet about this?"

"I have friends and family that I don't want to get hurt or killed. These people will kill anyone to protect their secrets. I'm only alive now because Hector is afraid of what Sara would do to him if something happened to me. If that changes, they'll kill me as quickly as you would swat a mosquito, maybe quicker.

"If you care for your family, you'll drop this. Sara knows what she's doing. She's tough and smart. She'll settle this in some manner, or die trying. I don't think there's anything you can do to help her, all you'll do is endanger your own family. You may feel guilty about doing nothing, but Sara understands. She knows her enemy. She doesn't expect help. She wouldn't want you getting yourself, or your family killed. Trust me; she'll deal with this problem. She gave him a second chance after he tried to kill her before. I suspect she's not in that charitable of a mood anymore. She'll find him and she'll kill him, or make him wish he was dead. You don't mess with that girl."

* * *

That girl was now in western Montana. A series of rides from truckers and travelers had gotten her here. There was no paper trail showing where she was. She was at the edge of a ranch encompassing nearly a hundred square miles. The owner of the ranch had hired her to resolve a problem nearly ten years ago. The two had hit it off and had kept in occasional touch since that time. Shannon had spent some downtime in one of his outlying cabins from time to time and had an open invitation to return whenever she wanted to. It was here that she'd learned to use a sniper rifle. She loved it here. The mountain air, the wide-open spaces, and the solitude were what she needed now. She needed to get herself back into top shape, both mentally and physically and there was no place like this for doing so.

She'd placed a call to the owner of the property from a small town nearby, only to find that he was out of town. She made her way to the property anyway and hiked back to the cabin she'd used before. It was at the extreme western edge of the property and Shannon found it much as she'd left it the last time. She stocked the cupboards with the supplies she'd bought in town and soon had a fire going. For the next couple of days, she kept busy chopping firewood and organizing the cabin. It was while returning to the cabin with a load of logs that Shannon saw the two horsemen approaching the cabin. She slid into the shadows nearby and watched as the two men approached. She lowered her guard when she recognized the property owner.

"Hi, Charlie," called out Shannon as the men tied their horses to the fence in front of the cabin.

"Hey, Sara," said Charlie Strong calling her by the alias he knew. "I was hoping it was you up here. This here is my new ranch foreman, Julio."

"Morning, Julio," said Shannon nodding to the man who was frowning at her. "Hope you don't mind me using the cabin for a while? I called, but you were out of town."

"Not a problem," said Charlie. "Damn it, girl! I missed you! What have you been up to? I haven't heard from you in the last couple of years."

"It's been over five years. I got married and had a kid."

"You?" asked Charlie in disbelief.

"I fell in love. It happens you know."

"I know it all too well. Hell, I'm on wife four now. Did you bring them along with you?"

Shannon had to work for a second to suppress the tears that were welling up in her eyes.

"No. They got killed a while back. I needed to head someplace to get my head and body pulled back together."

Charlie saw Shannon fighting back the tears and dismissed Julio on a chore that would take him from the area. He waited until Julio had left and then approached Shannon.

"What happened?"

"Some guys tried to take me out. My husband and son got in the way. I got hit in the shoulder but I escaped."

"A former client?" asked Charlie already knowing the answer. Shannon nodded and Charlie muttered a curse or two before continuing. "Stay here as long as you want. Do you need anything, weapons, food, cash, anything?"

"I'm okay."

"Who was it? Who killed them?"

"They were pros working for a private security firm. The firm is Bentley Security. I'm pretty sure I know who they were working for, or at least on behalf of. I'll deal with it later. I need to get stronger now."

"Bentley Security?" asked Charlie.

"Do you know them?"

"Yes. They're a politically connected group of asses. Roger Bentley is the founder of the company. He's a self-aggrandizing piece of bull crap. He likes to project this image of himself as a cross between Rambo and James Bond. He's just an ass. If you believe him, he was in Special Forces in Nam and then worked as a private contractor all over the world doing dirty deeds. He wrote a book about his exploits in which he boasts about his deeds. People have tried to fact-check it and come up empty. It looks like pretty much everything he's ever said was a lie.

"Bentley Security controls half the prisons in the country. They also do international work. They're a bunch of thugs as much as anything. They hire people right out of prison and military rejects. They think they can get away with anything and they usually do."

"They'll learn."

"You're going to need an army to take them on," said Charlie. "Bentley Security is a monster. I can round you up some help if you'd like?"

"Sorry. This is personal. I can handle this. It won't be a problem. They've never had to deal with a threat like me. I need you to keep quiet on this Charlie. No one can know I'm here. I'm going to need some time to get myself pulled together. I let myself get a tad out of shape and I've got a shoulder to rehabilitate. Can I trust you to keep this quiet?"

"Consider it done. I'll stop by from time to time to see if you need anything. Wait a minute! What about a horse? I've got a new stallion that's a real handful. He could use some taming. I seem to recall you liking a wilder horse. You could use him and help me out at the same time. I've got to get him away from the mares anyway. You've got that small stable over there. How about it? I can have him up here with a bunch of feed in a matter of minutes."

"That sounds good, Charlie. I could use a horse for a while. Riding is good exercise."

"With this horse, you'll get more exercise picking yourself up from the ground after he throws you."

"I don't think that'll be much of a problem."

"I'll be back in a few minutes with him."

Shannon watched as Charlie got back on his horse and rode away. It took about an hour before she saw him coming back. Dancing around on the end of a rope behind Charlie and his horse was a magnificent stallion who looked none too happy, behind him was a pick-up truck driven by Julio filled with stuff in the back.

Shannon walked over to meet Charlie who threw the rope to the stallion to her.

"This guy should keep you busy while you're up here," said Charlie with a laugh as the stallion tugged at the rope.

Shannon walked up the rope to reach the head of the horse that flared his nostrils and stomped the earth. She reached out a hand and he backed away. She reached out again, this time limiting the free rope, and stroked his head for a few seconds before tying him to the fence and walking back to Charlie.

"I know you said you didn't need anything, but I thought I'd bring you a few supplies anyway," said Charlie nodding to the back of the pickup.

"Got you some feed for the horse, some grub for yourself. There's a cured ham and some bacon in there. There's a bunch of canned goods, a couple of cases of beer, a couple of bottles of wine. You remember Marley?"

"Your German shepherd?"

"Yeah. Would you like to keep him up here with you?"

"I'm not taking your dog from you, Charlie."

"You wouldn't have to. My wife has booted him out of the house after he ate a pair of her boots. He's just spending all of his time sulking in the barn now. I had Julio load him and some chow for him into the pickup. It would be helping me out if you'd keep him up here with you for a while until she calms down and I can get him back in the house. Besides that, he beats the hell out of any security system I can provide you with. He'll hear anything long before you ever do. Given your circumstances and all, it probably wouldn't hurt to have an extra pair of eyes and ears."

He opened the pickup door and out bounded Marley, ninety-plus pounds of very fit dog.

"Hey, boy!" called Shannon as Marley bounded to her. "You remember me, do you?"

The paws on the shoulder and face washing made it clear that he remembered her very well and considered her a friend.

"Okay, okay!" cried out Charlie. "That's enough of that you two! You can get to know one another better after I get out of here. We've got a truck to unload."

Shannon followed Charlie around to the back gate of the pickup and watched as he lowered it. Several items caught her eyes.

"Are you expecting trouble?" asked Shannon eyeing the gun cases and ammunition.

"Figured it would be smarter to be safe than sorry," said Charlie nodding to one of the gun cases. "You've got a brand new, one-of-a-kind fifty caliber smart rifle in this case along with a couple of lower powered rifles. The fifty-caliber rifle gives you a maximum range of over two miles and packs a hell of a punch. It automatically adjusts for wind, air temperature, elevation, and God only knows what else. The guy who made it is a computer genius. He used some sort of laser or something that bounces off the target and adjusts the rifle to hit whatever's in the crosshairs. It might come in handy if you see anyone heading this way from a distance. It also does a hell of a job on vehicles. You can take out an engine block with one shot. Word has it you can bring down a chopper should one come around. Don't know how you'd hold the damned thing up to do so, it weighs a ton, but that's what they say. I've got you a thousand rounds of ammunition for each gun, but the fifty caliber rifle, you only get two hundred rounds for him. Mind you they're armor-piercing and pack a hell of a punch. If you need more than that, then you've got a bigger problem.

"There are also ten special shells for that rifle. I wouldn't use them unless you have to. They've got a depleted uranium slug that can penetrate any armor made. They're also over-packed with propellant and have a few surprises built-in. The damned things will kill the gun after ten to twenty shots, but they're handy to have around. Anything that doesn't get stopped by the normal rounds will fall to those. They also have an enhanced range and amazing penetrating power. The only real issue is the damned things strip the rifling out of the barrel they move so fast. After ten to twenty shots of those rounds, at most, the rifle's a lost cause.

"This case has a sniper rifle, like the one I gave you before, and some handguns. You've got a couple of fully automatic handguns and a couple of semi-automatic pistols. You've also got a bunch of spare clips. There are also got a couple of shotguns should things develop close in. They might also come in handy if you want some fresh food anytime. I wouldn't go out much without at least some firepower close by. It can be kind of dangerous in these parts. You're never sure what you're going to run into."

"How big a weapons cache do you have?" asked Shannon as she buckled on a holster that Charlie was holding out.

"Enough to outfit a small army," said Charlie with a smile. "One can't have too many guns."

"They do come in handy at times."

"I'd rather have too many than not enough. Find yourself with too few one time and you end up dead. Come on; let's get this stuff unloaded so I can get out of here."

* * *

Celia Underwood arrived back in Virginia and stopped in her husband's office on her way home from the airport.

"I missed you," said Tommy Underwood as he greeted his wife. "Did you have a good trip?"

"It was okay," said Celia as Tommy led her into his office and closed the door.

"What did you find out?"

"The guy who tried to get Shannon killed when she was in Los Angeles was Hector Esteban."

"Hector Esteban?" asked her husband. "The Hector Esteban?"

"That's what Kevin Seales told me."

"I wasn't expecting that."

"It seems she killed his first wife for him and then turned up back in town when he was running for the Senate. They belonged to the same gym and Kevin showed him her photo while they were talking about women. Hector thought they were teaming up to blackmail him, so he hired some thugs to take them out. Shannon saw them and took them out first. She traced the thugs back to Hector and got everything stopped. Now it looks like everything is starting up again."

"Jesus!"

"Did anything happen here while I was gone?"

"Not much. The prints from the cabin and car match those we had of Shannon so she was probably there. We didn't find anything showing where she might have gone. The FBI can't give me anything definitive on the tires or shoe impressions from the Bentley group unless they see the originals and the originals were turned over to Bentley Security after the State Police finished with them and they're now out of reach. The guy I know in Jersey took a look at the images and said they looked suspicious to him, but that he'd need the originals to give a real opinion. He was pretty sure a couple of the impressions were a match, but he can't swear to it without the originals."

"Where does that leave us?"

"Legally, we don't have a lot to go on. Unless something big breaks our way, this is likely to end up just like it is now."

"And they get away with murder," muttered Celia.

"I'm not sure losing eight men counts as getting away with it. I suspect Shannon could be after the rest of them also. Their guys don't seem overly relaxed when we bump into them. I haven't heard of anything specific happening to them, but those guys are pretty tense when we encounter them. If she catches up to them then she'll make them pay, but there's not a lot left for us to do."

"I'm thinking that might not be such a bad thing. I wanted to help Shannon, but I don't know how we can."

"If she needs our help, she knows how to reach us," said Tommy.

CHAPTER SIX

For the next four months, Shannon spent her days running, climbing, cutting wood, and riding. The stallion had taken a couple of weeks to calm to the point where he was a reasonably comfortable ride, but he now excelled. Marley accompanied Shannon wherever she went. It wasn't unusual to see the three of them racing through the fields. All three were in peak condition when Shannon decided it was time to leave. Charlie stopped by that afternoon and found Shannon and Marley sitting outside the door to the cabin.

"You two look comfortable," said Charlie.

"I'm getting too comfortable. That's the problem. If I stay here any longer I won't ever want to leave."

"And that's bad because?"

"I've got business to take care of. I think I'll start heading back tomorrow. I'm ready to do what I have to do. I've been a burden on you long enough as it is."

"You may be a lot of things, but a burden isn't one of them. You've more than paid your way by taming that stallion. Mind you, I'm not quite sure I trust him all that much yet, but he's a hell of a lot better than he was. I'm not sure I've ever seen Marley looking any better. You've even chopped more wood than you've burned. Anytime you need a break, you drop in."

"Thanks, Charlie. I needed the time to get my head together and to get my body patched up."

"How's the shoulder feeling?"

"It's almost as good as new. It gets a little cranky first thing in the morning, but it loosens up pretty quickly. More importantly, my head is back working right. Much as I hate to say it, it's time I got out of here."

"I'm going to hate to see you go. I want you to come back to the house with me. I've got some things there for you."

"Things?"

"Good things," said Charlie with a smile. "You saddle up that stallion of mine and ride him down. I'll have everything set out for you."

Charlie rode back off towards the house and Shannon headed over to the barn to saddle up the stallion. She rode him back with Marley wandering along behind them. As she came out of the woods near the house, she caught sight of Charlie's surprise. She rode up to where he was standing and dismounted.

"What have you done?" asked Shannon.

"I bought you a going-away present," said Charlie nodding to the Mercedes Benz sports car with a large red bow he was standing in front of. "Bulletproof glass all the way around. It's got Kevlar and advanced ceramic composites shielding the critical areas. It should stop anything anyone's likely to throw at you. An RPG might ding it a bit, but I'm not sure one of those would even stop it. It took a lot of convincing to get the manufacturer to install this package in a sports car. They normally only do it for sedans. I never figured you for the sedan type of lifestyle though. The tires are incapable of going flat. They're filled with some special foam that simulates air but will handle the same even if the tires are punctured. They had to beef up the suspension of the car a tad to handle the extra weight of the armor, but the performance is still better than almost anything else on the road.

"I had them do a couple of body modifications also. There are some hidden areas in the frame where a rifle, even that fifty-caliber monster can be safely hidden. There are also a couple of hiding places for handguns that aren't there unless you know exactly where to look. There are even a couple of bins built into the back that hold tire spikes. You pull a hidden release under the dash and out they drop flattening the tires of whoever is behind you."

"Who do you think I am? James Bond?"

"You can't be too prepared. I know who you're gunning for. I have some feel for the problems you're going to run into. I want you kept alive and well. Anything I can do to help in that is a small price to pay."

"You've done too much," said Shannon walking around the car.

"There is one more thing," said Charlie holding out a large manila envelope.

"What's that?"

"Absolutely everything I could find out about Bentley Security and Roger Bentley. Plans to Roger Bentley's house, offices and everything I know and could find out about Bentley Security are in there. You've got a CD-ROM with schematics of the alarm system, surveillance system, and the entire layout of his places. I've even thrown in a few satellite shots of the neighborhood and some photographs of his home. There's a list of contracts Bentley has with various firms and agencies. There are reports from various investigations that have been done on Bentley

Security. Just about anything you want to know about them is in that file including plans for their headquarters."

"How did you get all of that?"

"Most of the stuff is more or less part of the public record. I pulled a few strings here and there to get some of it, but it might help you out. I've got a few friends here and there who have or can get access to just about anything. I have a guy who enjoys hacking computers and is damned good at it."

"How did you know I was targeting Bentley?"

"It makes sense. This is private between you and him. It's easier to handle private things in private. Now if you'll excuse me, I have to see if I can get Marley back in the house again. That is if he'll still have anything to do with me. Come on, boy! Let's go! You take care of yourself. If you need anything, you know where I am. Don't be afraid to call. I'll have some people in the area keeping an eye on things. If you need help on anything, and I mean anything, then give me a call and I'll get you what you need."

* * *

In Washington, the inauguration of Hector Esteban had been the big story. Hector had won the election with fifty-one percent of the vote. There was grumbling from the right that the press had handed the election to Hector with their coverage of Eleanor's illness, but he wasn't about to complain.

"Congratulations, Hector," said Roger Bentley raising his glass of champagne.

"I wasn't sure I'd win it, but the party came through for me," said Hector.

"With the media on our side, we were able to pull this off. Their focus on Eleanor's health and condition made her something of a martyr for the party."

After a few more minutes of congratulations, the conversation took a less pleasant turn.

"Have you had any word on our missing friend?" asked Hector.

"She's either gone deep underground or is already dead. Don't worry about her. She can't hurt you now. If she was going to do something it would have been during the campaign. We're still working on finding her, but she's learned from her past mistakes and we're having a harder time tracking her. We've found a couple of truckers who claim they took her west after she killed our guys, but we've lost track of her after that. The murder of the eight men in the motel ruined her ability to get close to you. Those murders meant that we could turn loose every police department in the country to look for her. If she's still alive she'll turn up and when she does, we'll eliminate her."

"But you're still looking for her?"

"We don't want her running around loose any more than you do. We know how dangerous she is. We're just waiting for her to pop her head above ground and then we'll cut it off. She won't be a problem. She's either hiding someplace or dead and we'll eventually find her. She can't hide forever. We'll find her and we'll kill her when we do. But for now, let's celebrate your win and look to the future."

* * *

The trip east had given Shannon plenty of time to examine the materials Charlie had given her. He'd saved her a week or so of research and had probably exceeded what she could have learned on her own. Some of what she'd learned was to be expected, but some of the things had come as a surprise. The ten-foot-tall stone and concrete wall surrounding the estate had been higher and stronger than she'd expected. There had been some complaints from neighbors about the wall, but Shannon was surprised to see that the community had allowed him to build the wall. She was also surprised to find only one way into and out of the compound. While it minimized the number of gates and made limiting entry easier, it also served to trap anyone inside with only one escape route. That could come in handy down the road.

The satellite photos were especially interesting as they showed the security guards patrolling inside the walls. In the photos she had, there were always six men on foot patrolling inside the gates with dogs and another team at the gate checking vehicles that attempted to enter. A chicane had been erected out of large concrete blocks that forced any vehicle attempting to enter to travel slowly to pass through. The plans showed bulletproof glass used for every window. The security patrols would make life difficult.

Shannon knew that she needed to see the estate firsthand to develop a plan on how to proceed. She found a spot on a nearby hillside that overlooked the sprawling estate of Roger Bentley. From this vantage point, she could observe the comings and goings from the compound and the activity within the compound.

Shannon spent several days observing the compound below her. Getting entry into this place would be a challenge. Breaching the wall was nearly impossible. Even if one were able to breach the wall one would still need to dash across a well-patrolled open area to reach the house. While not impossible, the surveillance cameras or foot patrols would surely catch her if she tried that. Driving in and directly challenging the guards, would gain entry, but it would also alert the people inside, and with heavily armored panic rooms on each floor, it was imperative to sneak in unnoticed to prevent the targets from getting to a safe location. Finding a way in was going to be challenging.

She observed everything that went on in the compound including the arrival and departure of the staff. There was a hope that she could sneak in hidden in a vehicle, but every vehicle, even those of Roger Bentley and his wife, was examined upon entering the chicane. The trunks were opened and the seating area of every vehicle was examined. Even the underside of every vehicle was checked with a wheeled mirror that allowed the operator to look under the vehicle.

The sun was starting to set one evening when Shannon noticed a glint of sunlight reflecting off of something running from the woods near the road towards the estate. She focused the binoculars on the object and noted the cable running towards the house. The cable ran straight across the wide-open space without appearing to sag.

"Why doesn't it sag?" Shannon asked herself. "That's a long run, but no sag whatsoever." She decided to investigate further and made her way down the slope towards the wooded area where the cable originated.

The mystery of the cable was soon solved. At the very corner of the property, the telephone lines and cable television lines went from the road to a pole that was embedded in the ground directly adjacent to the fence. This pole was also secured by two heavy guy wires that ran back from the pole and the fence. The pole was a good forty feet tall. It was nearly hidden by the trees growing around it. The lines that left the street sloped up to reach the top of the pole where they then ran towards the house.

Shannon looked up the pole and noticed that there was a heavy steel cable running from the top of this pole to the estate and the telephone and TV cables were then secured to that cable. The steel cable running towards the house appeared to be much stronger than necessary to carry the weight of the cables. Shannon retreated up the hill to a position where she could see over the wall to see where the cables entered the house.

From this spot, Shannon could see the cable was secured to a heavy eyebolt embedded in the masonry of the large chimney on that end of the house. The smaller cables carrying the telephone and cable signals then entered the house through an attic vent. Shannon examined the attic vent. She then surveyed the location of the surveillance cameras and a smile came to her face. She knew how to get in.

* * *

Isabella Rodriguez was heading upstairs to deliver Mimi Bentley's breakfast. Isabella had been Mimi's maid for nearly twenty years now. The two had formed a close bond and Isabella looked after Mimi as though she were her daughter. Her high regard did not extend to Roger Bentley. The fact that most of her information came from Mimi no doubt colored her judgment of the man, but to Isabella, Mimi was a saint who had married a snake. Roger's disregard for anyone lower than him in social status had made him the enemy of the staff. Mimi Bentley on the other hand never failed to ask about them and their families. Every birthday, anniversary, or other celebration was noted by Mimi with an appropriate gift.

This day was not going well for Isabella. She had arrived this morning to find that someone had taken one of the chef knives from the drawer where she kept them. She had questioned other staff members about this, but all had denied any knowledge. A search of the area had not turned up the knife and Isabella was annoyed. On top of that, the coffee maker had chosen this morning to act up. Isabella had been forced to use instant coffee for Mimi's breakfast and she knew that would displease her mistress. Mimi loved her fresh brewed coffee and Isabella would make certain that a new coffee maker was in place by tomorrow morning.

As Isabella carried the tray up the stairs she glanced under the door and was surprised to see the room was still dark. Surely they weren't both still asleep? She set the tray down on the table alongside the door and knocked lightly. No one answered. Isabella checked the door and found it unlocked. She opened it a bit and looked into the bedroom. What she saw brought a blood-curdling scream from her lips that had everyone in the house running towards her.

The first person to reach her was one of the younger maids who saw the stricken look on Isabella's face and froze.

"Call an ambulance!" screamed Isabella at the girl. "Call them now! Miss Mimi is hurt!" she screamed. The girl pulled a cell phone from her pocket and immediately started dialing.

Gregory Butler was the next person on the scene. He was in charge of household security for the Bentley estate. His office was downstairs adjacent to the entry and he hurried upstairs at the sound of the scream. The young maid ran past him down the stairs with the phone to her ear as he made his way to where Isabella was standing with a stricken look on her face.

"What is it?" demanded Gregory. "What's wrong?"

"Miss Mimi..." muttered Isabella pointing into the room.

Gregory moved Isabella aside and opened the bedroom door. In the dim light of the room, he could see the two forms lying in bed. Blood covered the bedding on the left side of the bed and Mimi lay under the bedding staring up at the ceiling with the blank expression of the dead. Next to her lay her husband with a bloody chef knife in his right hand, apparently asleep and unhurt but with blood covering his arm and hand.

Gregory entered the room and flicked on the overhead lights. Roger Bentley flinched at the bright light and rolled onto his side. Gregory hurried to his side and touched his shoulder. Roger Bentley glared up at him and muttered, "What is it?"

"Are you alright, sir?" asked Gregory.

"I'm fine," muttered Roger Bentley. "Now get out and let me get back to sleep!"

"Sir," said Gregory gently. "We've got to get you out of here! We've got to get you out of here now!"

Roger Bentley opened his eyes once more and raised his right hand to point at his chief of security and order him out. It was only then that he became aware of the knife in his hand.

"What the hell?" asked a confused Roger Bentley seeing the knife and blood. "Am I hurt?" he asked in a panic quickly examining himself. It was only then that he noticed the body of his wife.

"You killed her!" screamed Isabella who had now ventured into the room and was staring at the body of her beloved mistress. "You killed Miss Mimi!"

"We've got to get you out of here, sir," said Gregory once more reaching down to take the arm of Roger Bentley.

Roger pulled away from the grasp and looked at the knife in his hand. The knife was stuck to his hand from the dried blood and Roger had to pry it from his hand before he dropped it on the bed like it was on fire.

"What the hell happened?" asked Roger confusedly, staring from the body of his wife to the knife and then up at the crowd in the room that was rapidly growing as more and more staffers came rushing in.

"We've got to get you out of here, sir," said Gregory. "We can figure out what happened later, but for now we've got to get you someplace safe. We've got to get you out of here."

"That's where you're wrong," said a new voice. Gregory looked back to see a police officer had entered the room carrying a first aid bag followed by another officer with an oxygen tank. "This is a crime scene. No one is to touch anything." He looked to the other officer who was already on the radio calling for more help.

"Did you check for a pulse?" asked the police officer nodding towards the body of Mimi Bentley.

"I didn't think it was really necessary," said Gregory.

"It's not," agreed the officer. "But, this is a crime scene and I need to know exactly who's touched what in here."

"Why are you here?" asked Gregory. "I didn't call the police."

"The dispatcher got a 911 call for an ambulance," explained the officer. "We were just down the road, so we came in with the oxygen and defibrillator hoping to help. Your guys at the front gate can verify that. They let us in. Now, I want everyone to follow my partner here downstairs. I don't want any of you talking among yourselves. I don't want anyone talking to anyone. Is that understood? I need statements from everyone and I don't need you all talking among yourselves first."

Everyone but Roger Bentley, the police officer, and Gregory filed out of the room.

"Care to tell me what happened here, sir?" asked the police officer taking his notepad out of his pocket.

"I don't know," muttered Roger Bentley looking at his dead wife and the knife that had been in his hand. "I just don't know."

"I'd rather he wasn't questioned until his attorney is present," said Gregory. "He's obviously in shock right now and is in no position to be questioned. It is probably best that none of the staff is questioned until we get some legal representation here."

"What you want doesn't matter," said the police officer. "This is a crime scene. There's been a murder here. The detectives are on their way. I'm betting you're going to get a lot of them. Does this house have an alarm system?"

"Of course," said Gregory. "It has the best system in the world. We've got surveillance cameras, thermal imaging, plus every bell and whistle you could ask for. There's also a twelve-person security detail in place twenty-four hours a day."

"We'll want the tapes from the surveillance cameras," said the officer. "Are there any in this room?"

"No," said Gregory. "This is a private part of the house. Only the public areas and the exterior are under surveillance."

"Were there any unauthorized visitors last night?" asked the officer.

"Not that I know of and I would know if there had been any."

"How many people were in the house last night?"

"I'd have to check the logs to know exactly, but it shouldn't have been more than five or six. We keep the number of personnel low overnight. The security patrol would have numbered twelve, but they would have stayed outdoors. There's usually a cook who works nights, a maid, and a secretary, plus Mr. and Mrs. Bentley. During the day that number goes up quite a bit, but overnight there shouldn't have been more than five or six people in the house."

"That limits the numbers of suspects," said the officer. "Are those people still here?"

"The overnight staff is gone. They were replaced by the daytime staff."

"We'll need their names and addresses," said the officer. There was a knock at the bedroom door and four men dressed in suits were standing there. The first of the detectives had arrived.

* * *

Hector Esteban was sitting in the upstairs private dining area of the White House sipping coffee and looking through the newspapers when an ad caught his eye. He froze and stared at the ad for several seconds.

"In loving memory of my beloved husband Jack Brewer, son Tyler Brewer, Gabrielle, and Miriam. Justice will be done!" read the ad.

Hector read the ad four times before putting down the paper and reaching for the phone. "Who the hell was Miriam?" was the thought that kept echoing through his brain as he dialed his father-in-law to advise him of the ad.

The phone rang for several seconds before it was answered.

"Hello?" asked a strange voice.

"Is Roger Bentley there?"

"I'm afraid he's busy right now," said the detective who'd answered the phone.

"This is President Esteban," said Hector. "I have to talk to him."

"I'm afraid that's not possible right now, sir," said the detective. "He's currently on his way to the police station for questioning in a murder investigation. I wouldn't count on talking to him anytime soon."

"Murder?"

"He's your father-in-law?" asked the detective finally putting the names together.

"That's right."

"We believe he killed his wife last night."

"Mimi's dead?" asked Hector finally connecting the name to the ad.

"She was stabbed to death with a kitchen knife last night. Members of the household staff found her husband asleep in bed alongside her with the knife still in his hands. Our interviews with the staff indicate that they've argued frequently recently and their relationship was deteriorating. We're still investigating everything, but it looks like a pretty open and shut case."

"He didn't kill her. I'm sure of that."

"Well, we'll see where the investigation leads, but right now he's the prime suspect."

* * *

Word spreads fast when crime strikes the rich and powerful. Right behind the detectives were the first news reporters. Within an hour, word of the murder had leaked out and coverage of it had taken over the cable news channels along with the local channels in the area.

Helicopters vied with each other for prime viewing angles as more and more investigators arrived. It didn't take long for the first news channel to report that Roger Bentley was considered the prime suspect in his wife's death. The video of him being removed from the estate in the back of an unmarked police car was soon airing repeatedly.

This video brought out different emotions in those who saw it. Shannon Brewer watched with amusement, while Hector Esteban watched with disbelief. His wife was devastated by the death of her mother, but Hector was more upset by the ad in the paper.

Craig Burke watched the news with absolute disbelief. He contacted those who'd worked the security detail the night before as soon as they were released by the police and saw to it that they were kept under watch. He found it inconceivable that Roger had anything to do with this death. He knew that had Roger wanted his wife dead that it could have been accomplished with little or no personal risk. He was confused as to what had happened, but he was going to personally find out who had done this. He acquired copies of the surveillance tapes and was still tracking down the last members of the household staff when the call from Hector Esteban came in.

"I'm sorry about your mother-in-law," said Craig Burke.

"She did it!" muttered Hector into the phone. "That bitch killed Mimi!"

"Who did it?" asked Craig grabbing a pen and paper to jot down the name.

"Shannon Brewer!" screamed Hector. "Who the hell do you think?"

"It wasn't her," said Craig setting down the pen. "It had to be someone on the staff or someone who was already in the house. I've seen the surveillance videos and no one else entered the house. No one left the house afterward either. The house has been under total surveillance and whoever did this was someone on the inside. We've searched the house top to bottom and there's no one else there. We've even gone through the house with thermal scanners and no one else is hiding there."

"You didn't see the paper today?" asked Hector. "Do you have a copy of the Journal there?"

"Right in front of me," said Craig as he pulled the paper to him and started to leaf through it.

"Look at page six."

"I see it," said Craig. He then emitted a long string of curses.

"We've got to tell the authorities. They think he did it. They're not even looking for anyone else. We've got to turn them on to her."

"We can't tell the authorities. What do we say? We tried to kill her and she's holding a grudge? If she did this, and yes, I said if, we'll have to hope she'll have left some sort of evidence. We just have to hope that it's found. If the investigators don't find it, then we have to find it."

"She killed eight of your guys and left no evidence."

"Yeah. She's good. I've got guys working side-by-side with the locals on this investigation and from what I've heard, all of the evidence points to someone within the household. Nothing unusual has turned up. Do we want the authorities looking at her? She mentioned Gabrielle's name in the ad. Do we want the authorities looking back at your first wife's death?"

"No!" insisted Hector. "But this had to be her. This fits her perfectly. She took out the ad to taunt us. She mentioned Gabrielle to threaten me."

"Why would she kill Mimi and not Roger? He's the guy who ordered the hit."

"Killing him would be too easy. This way she destroys him. He's accused of killing his wife. All of the evidence points at him. Even if he gets acquitted, the scar will follow. She threatened to do something like that with me. It's what she does."

"I've got to check up on this. Keep your cool for a while. Let me send some people to check up on who placed the advertisement. Maybe there's a trail from there. The ad had to be placed before the killing, so Sara knew she could succeed. I also want to take a closer look at the house and see if there's anything we might have overlooked regarding entry into the house. If we can find another way into the house, then maybe that will lead us to her, or some evidence she left behind. I just don't know how anyone could get in undetected past our security."

* * *

"Are you watching this?" asked Celia Underwood as soon as her husband answered the phone.

"Hello, to you too," said Tommy as he picked up the remote to his office television and turned on the television. "What channel should I be watching?"

"Pick almost any news channel. Everyone's covering it."

"Okay," said Tommy. He watched the feeds for a few seconds before speaking. "How does this affect us?"

"The house they're showing belongs to Roger Bentley. He's the head of Bentley Security among other things. They're claiming that he killed his wife."

"It happens," said Sheriff Underwood.

"I bet he didn't do it. I'll bet it was Shannon."

"That's a leap."

"Not really. She made her living by killing spouses and making it look like an accident leaving no trail behind her. How hard would it be to kill someone and make it look like murder with the husband being the murderer? She'd certainly have a motive."

"Why kill the wife and not the man himself?"

"She's trying to hurt him. She wants him to suffer. She wants him to suffer like she's suffered. Killing him would be too easy. She might end up killing him, but she's going to make him suffer first."

"You could be right," mused Tommy. "It would make some sense. It looks like a fort they were living in. How do you suppose she got in?"

* * *

That same question was first and foremost in the mind of Craig Burke as he walked through the house for the third time. Every staff member known to be in the house had now been cleared of involvement. Only Roger Bentley was still unable to account for what had happened and he wasn't talking on the advice of his attorney. This was rapidly becoming an open and shut case for the police and the local prosecutor. Unless Craig could turn something up, and do it soon, his boss would most likely be charged with this crime and barring a bizarre jury verdict, convicted.

It was while checking the locks on one of the third-floor windows for the third time that he first noticed the cables running over the wall and to the house. He hurried downstairs and looked up. He followed the cables over to the wall and then looked back at the house. The cables were secured to the chimney and then disappeared into the attic vent. Two members of his security detail were following him.

"Get me a long ladder," said Craig to one of the men.

"How long?" asked the man.

"Long enough to get me up there," said Craig pointing up to the chimney. It took several minutes before an appropriate ladder could be found and positioned. Craig swiftly climbed to the top and examined the cable and the vent. He grabbed the cable bundle and pulled down on it. It barely flexed at all with nearly his full weight on it. He stepped down on the ladder until the cable bundle was just within reach. He reached up and grabbed the bundle with both hands and lifted himself off the ladder. The cable held his weight without trouble. He hung there for several seconds looking across the span between where he was now and the wall, calculating if he could travel the distance hand over hand. He decided he could and started to climb hand over hand towards the pole where the cable originated. About halfway there, he started to question his judgment as his hands and arms were burning, but he knew that failure was not an option. The trip back was as long as the trip ahead and dropping off would surely result in serious injury if not death, so he quickened his pace.

After what seemed like forever, he reached the pole outside the wall and wrapped his arms and legs around it while his men hurried out from the compound with the ladder. Once back down the ladder and back on solid ground Craig hurried to the security room where the feeds from the surveillance cameras were recorded.

"Did you see me?" asked Craig to the guard who was monitoring the feeds.

"I saw you climbing the ladder, but then you disappeared."

"Replay the feeds from ten minutes ago," ordered Craig.

He watched the screens with intense interest for several minutes as the scene showed him climbing the ladder and then disappearing. He remained out of sight for the entire trip outside of the compound.

"Son of a bitch!" muttered Craig. "That's how she got in!"

"Who?" asked one of the guards.

"The woman who murdered Mrs. Bentley," answered Craig. "I want a light and camera added and focused on that wire by tonight. Are the police investigators still here?"

"Yes, sir," said the guard. "I believe they're down in the kitchen looking things over one final time."

Craig Bentley hurried from the room and found the last two investigators who were still in the house.

"I might have found something," said Craig.

He led the two men outside and explained what he'd done. He pointed them to the vent and advised them that it appeared to be easily removable. He urged them to go up there and investigate the area.

"Are you serious?" asked the lead investigator. "Do you think someone risked their neck to climb hand over hand along that wire to kill this guy's wife?"

"You either investigate it now or explain in court why you didn't," said Craig. "It's a way for a person to gain entry into the house without appearing on any of our cameras, or tripping any of the alarms. If the person I suspect is behind this, she might have left evidence behind. There might be a fingerprint, hair, or something that can pin this on her."

"Who do you think did this?" asked the investigator.

"There's a woman from the area who murdered eight of our men a while back. She thinks we're responsible for the death of her husband and son and she wants vengeance. I'm betting it was her."

"Have you told this to the detectives heading the investigation?" asked the investigator.

"Not yet. I had to find a way for someone to gain entry to the house. Without that, there's no way she could have pulled this off. That cable bundle is the way into the compound. I suspect she removed the vent from the wall and that got her inside the house. Once inside the house, she carried out the crime and then escaped the same way. There currently are no security cameras in the attic or alarm sensors. Those are two weaknesses that will be addressed by this evening. The attic stairs open into the upstairs hallway where once again there are no security cameras or alarm sensors since it's the Bentleys' private space. It's how she got in and got out. I'm sure of it."

The investigator looked up at the cable bundle and the vent before replying. "Hell of a lot of work to go through to kill a guy's wife. We'll take a look, but I bet we don't find anything. I think you're grasping at straws here, but we'll take a look."

Craig stood back and watched as the two men made their way shakily up the ladder, retracing his steps. The men examined the vent intently for several minutes and then climbed back down and made their way over to where Craig was waiting.

"We've looked the vent over from outside and nothing looks out of place," said one of the investigators. "There aren't any obvious fingerprints or trace evidence. It's screwed into the wall and the screws appear normal. It could have been removed or it may not have been touched since it was installed. We can't tell. There's nothing obvious going on up there. We're going to head inside and take a look from the inside. We'll examine the attic and see if anything jumps out, but it looks like your boss is going to have to answer for this. I don't think it's reasonable to assume that anyone gained entry that way."

"It's the only way into the house that wasn't monitored," said Craig. "It's doable. That's how she got in."

"We'll see what turns up. But, right now, I don't see that being a very likely option. You might as well argue that a ghost materialized and killed her and then disappeared. For anyone to traverse that span across a well-lit yard that's patrolled by security and then pop off a vent and move about inside, kill a woman and then escape the same way all without leaving a sign, or being detected, is asking a lot. I just don't see that happening."

"It happened."

"Who is this woman? Superwoman?"

"Something like that," muttered Craig as he looked back up at the vent once more.

* * *

Roger Bentley was not having a good day. He felt hung-over and he was beginning to suspect it wasn't just the shock that made him feel that way. He was now sitting in an interview room at the local police station waiting for the detectives to come back once more. It was now six hours since he'd been awakened. His attorney, Jason Wood was sitting beside him having been summoned earlier. Roger looked around the room and tried to remember what had happened last night, but it was all a blur. Had he murdered Mimi? He'd killed before, but he'd always done so with a purpose and usually from a distance. Why would he have killed Mimi, and why didn't he remember it if he did? Was he sane? He smiled at that question remembering what a psychology professor had once said during college. "Crazy people don't ask if they're sane. They just assume they're sane. If someone asks you if they're sane, they almost certainly are. It's the ones who know they're sane that you have to worry about. They're usually not."

Roger's attorney had his cell phone glued to his ear and was taking notes as Roger pondered his situation. Roger glanced at the notes the attorney was taking and then grabbed the notepad from the table.

"What the hell?" asked Roger reading the notes. "Where did you get this?"

The lawyer hung up the phone and then took back the paper from Roger.

"That was Craig Burke I was talking to. He said that there was an ad placed in a local paper that may be useful in exonerating you. I was just writing down the information. Does it mean anything to you?"

"It was her? Thank God! It was her! It wasn't me! Jesus! It wasn't me!"

"Who was it?"

"There's a woman who killed some of our men a while back. Her name is Shannon Brewer. She'd disappeared after that. We've been looking for her."

"She might be back. Mr. Burke thinks he's found out how she got into the compound and possibly into the house without being noticed. The police are looking into it. We're going to have our guys follow up on it too. With any luck, we might get something to help exonerate you."

For the first time all day, Roger felt relieved. There was light at the end of the tunnel and it wasn't a train coming at him. He might get out of this mess. All they had to do was find the woman they hadn't been able to find and then get her to confess to the crime. That light suddenly started to dim as he considered the problem.

How the hell do you do that? Finding Shannon had proven impossible. She'd now apparently managed to come back to the region undetected and carry out a murder in one of the most securely guarded estates in the country and escape without leaving much, if any trail. And now his only chance for freedom lay with finding her and pinning the murder on her. Add in the weight of evidence against him, the bloody knife with his prints on it, the arguments he and Mimi had, his inability to account for what happened, and the lack of anyone else showing up on the surveillance, and Roger's chances of ever walking free again weren't so great. The relief flowed away and depression swept in once again.

"We're not going to find her," said Roger.

"Don't give up," said the attorney. "If she's behind this, then we'll find her. I'll hire an investigator who'll track her down."

"It's not that simple. I've had twelve teams of investigators looking for her for the last four months. She's not that easy to find. This girl is a pro. She's a damned ghost when she wants to be. Now, not only do we have to find her, but we have to get her to admit to what she's done while at the same time keeping quiet about other things she was involved with. She's not going to be willing to implicate herself just to exonerate me."

"What other things has she been involved with?"

"I can't go into that here. Suffice to say we don't necessarily want her telling everyone everything she knows. That might be worse than having her stay quiet. What happens if we don't find her?"

"If not, all we need is one juror on our side and we win. All it takes is reasonable doubt. I believe you'll be charged with first-degree murder. Finding you with the knife in your hands pretty much makes that a given. There aren't any good plea bargain options out there, so unless we can get you exonerated, this will probably go to trial."

"What kind of plea bargain could we offer?"

"There's nothing that would help us. A plea in a case like this normally would start with the prosecutor offering fifty years with no parole and we'd probably eventually settle on somewhere around twenty-five years. Twenty-five years would be too long for you. You probably can't expect to survive more than twenty years in prison and there's no chance that the prosecutor would accept twenty years. Not with the evidence, there seems to be against you. Your security precautions are killing you now. Without someone else showing up on the surveillance cameras, without the alarms tripping, without the guards catching someone, the focus has to be on those within the house. Even if this information about this woman pans out, the prosecutor will think you were an active participant. They found you sleeping alongside your dead wife with the bloody knife in your hand. I'm going to have to work very hard to get a juror on our side. It's not impossible, but it won't be the easiest case I've ever argued."

* * *

Just how hard that case would be was made clear during the bail hearing later that evening. The prosecutor addressed the judge and laid out the bare bones of the case against Roger Bentley.

"Your honor," said the prosecutor. "Miriam Bentley was found murdered in her bed this morning with her husband Roger Bentley asleep by her side with the presumed murder weapon in his right hand. All of the evidence points to Mr. Bentley being the sole assailant in this case. We've examined the surveillance videos from the property and they show no unauthorized persons entering the estate. Those who were on the property can account for their activities during the time in question. Only Mr. Bentley has been unable to account for his actions.

"The murder weapon was taken from a drawer in the kitchen. The surveillance cameras in the house were controlled from Roger Bentley's bedroom and the ones monitoring the kitchen area were turned off for about five minutes before being turned back on. Fingerprints on the console controlling the cameras match only Roger Bentley.

"Fingerprints on the murder weapon match only Mr. Bentley. There are no unexpected fingerprints found in the bedroom or evidence of any kind indicating an alternative killer. It is as apparent as possible that Roger Bentley decided to kill his wife. He then turned off the surveillance cameras showing the kitchen area as he gathered the murder weapon. He turned back on those cameras after retrieving the knife. He then stabbed his wife to death before returning to bed. We are filing charges of murder in the first degree. We request that the defendant be held without bail."

"Mr. Wood?" asked the judge.

"Your honor," began Jason. "We are confident that Mr. Bentley will ultimately be exonerated of these charges. We are currently examining an alternative point of entry that was probably used by the true perpetrator of the crime that would bypass the surveillance videos and alarm system. We are confident that the true perpetrator of this crime will soon be determined and Mr. Bentley exonerated."

"Your honor," interjected the prosecutor. "Their alternative entry point has been examined by the detectives and while it's conceivably possible that a person could have gained entry by that means, there is no evidence that anyone did, and the detectives in the case consider it extremely unlikely that this was, in fact, the entry point. Every piece of evidence that's been recovered to this point implicates Mr. Bentley."

"Your honor," continued Jason Wood. "This rush to indict my client is indicative of a problem in the criminal justice system. Once the police have identified a likely suspect, they tend to focus almost exclusively on that person. My client is a good husband and father who did not murder his wife. He is one of the victims in this case and deserves compassion. We would urge you to release him on any reasonable bail."

"Your honor," countered the prosecutor. "In Mr. Bentley's autobiography, he boasts on at least four occasions of killing people and of his ability to slip out of various countries using aliases and false documents to escape prosecution. His corporation is officially listed as having nearly a hundred private aircraft. Given the overwhelming mass of evidence against him and the personal fortune he has amassed, it is not unreasonable to assume that he would attempt to flee the country, as he has claimed to have fled others seeking to prosecute him. Given the number of highly armed guards he employs and his assets. there is no way to guarantee his availability for a trial. He boasts in his autobiography of being a wanted man in multiple countries and laughs at their attempts to reach him. He is not someone we can assume will stay in reach."

"Your honor," countered Jason. "My client may have overstated some of his accomplishments in an attempt to boost book sales. To the best of my knowledge, he is not now wanted in any country and is not resisting extradition or prosecution. All he wants is a fair trial where the facts can be brought out in the open. He is now an older man who would suffer undue hardships if forced to stay in prison. Given the state of many of the prisons, it is not unreasonable to state that his very survival may depend on your setting a fair bail."

"Regarding his ability to survive in prison," countered the prosecutor. "I should point out that his security firm is currently the provider of prison guards to two of the prisons in this area. The only prison that his firm is not affiliated with is the old county jail which is still manned by county workers. I would like to recommend that he be remanded to that prison to limit his ability to get favorable treatment from guards who are also his employees."

"That is absurd! My client would not seek out or accept favorable treatment from the guards. The county jail is not fit for human habitation. It has been cited on multiple occasions and is not close to meeting the national standards for prisoner care. It should also be noted that my client recently attempted to acquire the contract for running that facility and harsh words were exchanged on both sides. Both the guards and the warden of the county jail have made statements that are openly hostile towards my client. Incarcerating him in that environment is tantamount to cruel and unnecessary punishment!"

"I think I've heard enough gentlemen," said the judge. "As to the bail, I must say that I am concerned about Mr. Bentley's willingness to face up to the charges facing him. I fear there is no bail that I can set that would be an undue hardship for him to lose in exchange for freedom, therefore I am refusing to set bail at this time. If evidence comes forward that implicates a second person, then we can revisit the bail issue, but until that happens, there will be no bail. Regarding the site of the incarceration, I must admit that I feel some uneasiness about having Mr. Bentley being guarded by his employees. There are too many ways that such a situation could be abused. Therefore, I am ordering him to be held in the county jail. I will forward a message to the warden and guards advising them to treat him exactly like they do other inmates and to not punish, or harass Mr. Bentley in any way. I will not tolerate his being treated in any manner other than that of every other inmate."

"That was a disaster," muttered Roger Bentley to his attorney after the hearing.

"I don't think we could expect anything different," said Jason Wood. "Hopefully our people will find some evidence to pin on this other woman and then we can get you out of there. In the meantime, I'll be there to see you on a routine basis and try to keep you as far from the regular inmates as possible. Just hang in there. We'll get through this."

CHAPTER SEVEN

Sheriff Tommy Underwood was sitting in his office going over paperwork when his secretary came in and closed the door behind her and walked over to his desk.

"There's a guy here who's a private investigator," said the secretary. "He wants to know if you're free to talk to him for a few minutes."

"Any idea what it's about?" asked Tommy.

"He said it involved Shannon Brewer."

"Okay. Send him in."

Tommy pulled an audio recorder from his desk drawer and set it on the desk. His secretary ushered the man into his office.

"Sheriff Underwood," said the secretary. "This is Hugo McBride."

The two exchanged greetings and then sat down on opposite sides of the desk.

"If you don't mind," said the sheriff. "I'll just record our conversation so there's no miscommunication or misunderstanding." He reached forward and turned on the recorder.

"No problem," said the investigator taking in the small tidy office.

"Now, what can I do for you?" asked the sheriff.

"I'm working with the legal team representing Roger Bentley. Some associates of his have mentioned their belief that Shannon Brewer was involved in the events leading up to his arrest. I've been advised that you were investigating her in regards to the murder of eight men in this county. I was hoping you could give me some information on that investigation."

"That's currently an open investigation so I can't tell you too much. I can tell you that we have no evidence at all implicating Shannon Brewer other than the unfounded suspicions of some of the employees of Bentley Security. We found no trace evidence of any kind implicating her. No fingerprints, no hair, no DNA, nothing. The room wasn't wiped clean. There were fingerprints galore of each of the sixteen people who had shared those rooms, but none matching hers. Even the digital photographs of the dead men only had their prints on them. There was no hair and other trace evidence found at the site linking her to the crime. If she was there, she left no detectable trace behind. Whoever committed those murders was either one of those in the room or was very, very careful and left us nothing in the form of evidence."

"Do you think she did it?"

"I honestly don't know. I knew Shannon for five years and I would never have guessed that she could do something like that. There are some indications that she played a role in it, but I find it hard to believe. Based on the evidence alone I would say it was one or more of the eight men that shared the hotel rooms with the eight who were murdered who committed the murders. Only their prints were in the room, but determining which one or which group has been impossible."

"You knew Shannon Brewer?"

"She married a guy who was my best friend. I saw them all the time. Shannon was the godmother of my children. I just don't see her doing some of the things they say she did. I've checked up on most of the claims the Bentley people made, but none of them have panned out."

"What have you checked on?"

"Nearly everything," said Sheriff Underwood. "Most of the cases they showed me were classified as natural deaths. After my calls, a couple of them were investigated again, but they found nothing to contradict the original findings and those cases are now closed. Her fingerprints supposedly matched those found at a couple of murder scenes. The problem is the eyewitness descriptions of the shooters don't come close to matching Shannon's physical description.

"In one case, the eyewitness has the shooter being a six-foot-two black male. In another case, the shooter was reported as being a six-foot Hispanic male. I can't find one case where the description of the shooter matches Shannon. She may have been at the crime scenes at some point, but that's about all you can say.

"I've talked to the detectives investigating each of these cases and they pretty much dismiss Shannon as being a suspect. They seem confused by the fingerprint match and would like to talk with her, but they don't consider her a suspect."

"That's what I've been hearing too. I've looked at pretty much everything related to her and none of it makes much sense."

Sheriff Underwood decided to do some fishing.

"Pretty much everything huh? There's a case from Los Angeles where someone killed four thugs. The original report seems to have been altered with lots of stuff deleted. I stumbled onto it when I ran her prints. I believe it might be related to her also."

"Los Angeles and four thugs? I don't think I've seen that case."

"You might want to give it a look. The guys who were killed were local thugs and no one misses them too much. One of the detectives I've talked to said that if she killed them, she should get a commendation and a medal. They seem to be leaning more towards it being gang-related."

"I'll look the case up. I wonder why I wasn't given it already? You said the prints matched?"

"Yeah. It's possible someone high up was involved in that case in some manner. She seemed to have a lot of higher-end clients."

"I've been hearing the same things," said the investigator. "She's had an interesting mix of clients if you believe all of the rumors. Either this girl is the best killer in the world, or we're all looking at the wrong person."

"Bentley Security sure seems to feel she's dangerous. I'm pretty sure they were responsible for ambushing her car and killing her husband and son and wounding her."

"Have you heard from her since then?"

"She called me a week or so later to tell me of the guys from Bentley Security at the motel and the others who were hiding around town. If it wasn't for that call I'd say she was an innocent victim in all of this. But in that call, I got the impression that she knew a lot more than she was letting on. I've heard some things since then that have me wondering how well I knew her."

"Would you care to elaborate?"

"I can't," said Tommy. If the people from Bentley didn't know that his wife had been in Los Angeles talking to people, he wasn't about to tip them off.

"I'll be honest with you. If my bosses weren't so adamant about her being involved in this event, I'd drop her like a rock. Nothing is pointing to her in this case, but everyone who's worked on finding her is sure she's behind this. I don't get it. They're saying she's doing it for revenge. I would think she'd kill Roger Bentley if that was her motivation. I just don't see her being behind this. You said the only fingerprints and evidence found in the murder of the eight men belonged to the Bentley employees?"

"That's right."

"You think it was one of the ones sharing the rooms that did the killing?"

"It would have to be two of them or one of those supervising them. The men in the field were working as two-man teams. Each man vouched for the other. We questioned everyone and no one jumped out at us. You're thinking the murderer might be an insider and not Shannon?"

"It makes as much sense as anything else. It makes more sense to me than some phantom girl. I can't find a link between the guys who were killed here and the guards at the house, but I suspect that's where this is going to end up."

"You don't think the old guy killed his wife himself?"

"I'm not going to answer that question with the tape recorder running. I've been told to assume that he wasn't responsible and that Shannon Brewer is the prime suspect."

"How could anyone get into that place? I was watching it on the news and the place looks like a castle. There's a giant wall, security guards, alarms, and surveillance cameras. I don't see how anyone could get in without being caught."

"That's why I suspect an inside job. The household staff has been cleared. They were all in the public part of the house and under surveillance the whole time. The security staff is all vouching for each other, but I don't know enough about them. Supposedly, there is a way in by shimmying across a hundred plus feet of cable and then removing an attic vent and climbing inside, but it's been looked at and there's no proof that anyone used that approach. I've been there and I've looked at it and you couldn't get me to try it without a gun at my head. That's one hell of a climb. One guy tried it and made it, but he barely made it and he's built like a linebacker. The guy's as strong as an ox and he could barely make it. I don't think anyone sane would try that approach. For a woman to make that climb would be pretty unlikely in my opinion. Then to be able to move through the house undetected and escape is asking a lot."

"Was it Craig Burke who made the crawl across the wire?" asked Tommy.

"How did you know that?"

"He was in the room when we found the bodies of his men. I kind of wondered if maybe he played some role in their murders. Do you know where he was when the Mimi Bentley murder went down?"

"I've tried to ask about him, but everyone keeps steering me back to Shannon Brewer."

"Why are they so focused on Shannon? Is it real, or are they using her as a diversion?"

"Damned if I know," said the investigator. "They seem to think she's some kind of ghost. I don't get it. You knew her. Was she that good?"

"As far as I know she was just a good wife and mother. Do you need anything else?"

"That's about it," said the investigator pulling a business card from his pocket. "If you find out anything that might help me, could you give me a call?"

"I'll do that. I trust you're done here?"

"I'm done," said the investigator with a smile. "I've heard you guys don't like people prowling about town."

"It's nothing personal. It's just that your employer tends to rub me the wrong way. I'm still pretty sure some of his people were responsible for the death of Jack Brewer and Tyler Brewer. I don't know if you've ever had a best friend gunned down in a field and left to die, but it tends to tick me off. Add in seeing your godchild still strapped into a child seat with half his head blown off and you can start to understand my displeasure with anyone associated with Bentley Security."

"You didn't have anything to do with the murder of Mrs. Bentley did you?" asked the investigator.

Tommy laughed before replying. "No. I wouldn't have killed his wife. If I'd played any role in this you'd be looking for the guy who killed him, not his wife. If he turns up dead anytime, then you can come looking for me. If I was investigating this, I'd be looking at Craig Burke. He's proven he can get into the house. He seems to turn up quite a bit when people die. Maybe it's all just a coincidence, but when someone keeps popping up like that, you've got to notice it."

The investigator read Tommy's response and it came across as being true. He shook hands and left the office. The investigation into Shannon Brewer was making no progress.

* * *

The desk clerk at the Baltimore hotel checked in the young woman who had appeared at the counter. He'd been surprised to see a security tag pop up alongside her name when he entered it into the computer. As per the rules for this tag, he'd continued with the check-in procedure as if nothing had happened and then he handed the key to her room to her. As she left the desk, he clicked on the contact tag and dialed the number that had been displayed. Within minutes of Shannon Brewer walking into the lobby of the hotel, word had reached the highest levels of Bentley Security of her arrival.

It took Craig Burke barely a half-hour from the time he'd received word of Shannon's arrival for him to reach the lobby of the hotel. The check-in clerk had been sequestered and was awaiting him. Craig removed a pile of photographs from his bag and spread them out in front of the man.

"Is she one of these women?" asked Craig Burke.

The man immediately pointed to one of the photos taken of Shannon during surveillance of her at her house before the attack.

"You're sure?" asked Craig as his four-man security detail waited behind him.

"That's her," said the man. "She's even wearing that same outfit. What did she do?"

"I can't tell you that. You said she was wearing the same clothes?"

"They look the same to me," said the clerk. "Even her hair was the same. You can see her on the security video from the lobby. She looks exactly like that."

Craig turned to talk to the head of hotel security that was standing nearby.

"Do we have that video?"

"I've got it cued up for you."

Craig watched the video and cursed as Shannon looked directly up into the security camera and smiled.

"Is she still in her room?" asked Craig.

"We believe so," said the employee of Bentley Hotel Security, a subsidiary of Bentley Security. It was the Bentley Hotel Security software that had identified Shannon Brewer. "We weren't notified immediately, but as soon as we were notified, we put the room under surveillance. We've also gone back and checked the surveillance videos and they don't show her leaving."

"I'm going to need a key to her room."

"I've already got it for you," said the head of hotel security holding out the keycard.

Craig took the card and then nodded towards his men. "My men and I'll take this from here. I want all of you to forget this ever happened. You never saw or reported anything. I have a computer guru who's ready to remove all traces of this from the computer log. We'll also take care of the video feeds. You saw nothing. You know nothing."

"Consider it forgotten," said the head of hotel security.

The check-in clerk nodded his agreement and Craig led his men from the room. The group moved up and into the hotel and then paused outside the door to Shannon's hotel room. Craig could feel the fear and tension rising in his body. This encounter had a bad feel to it. Shannon had disappeared for months and now suddenly reappeared in a hotel that was openly associated with Bentley Security. She'd registered under her name and hadn't altered her appearance. Not only had she not altered her appearance, but she'd also gone out of her way to dress identically to how she looked on a photo she knew they had and smiled into the security camera. Either she'd suddenly developed a death wish, or this was some sort of a trap. Craig doubted that she'd suddenly developed a death wish.

"We need her alive," whispered Craig to his security team checking to be sure that each man held their stun guns and not their side-arms.

Craig slid the keycard into the lock. His men flung the door open and poured into the room with Craig directly behind them. The room was empty except for an unsealed manila envelope sitting on the bed. Craig reached down and looked into the envelope and saw a DVD and a note inside the envelope and knew why Shannon had lured them here.

"She's not here," said one of his security team after searching the space.

"No," said Craig. "She just brought us here to give us this." He picked up the envelope and placed it inside his jacket. "Let's go. We've done what she wanted us to do."

"Why not mail it, or use one of the delivery services?" asked one of his men.

"Secretaries and underlings might intercept it. By doing it this way she'd be sure it got into the right hands. She's a clever girl, perhaps too clever. Let's get back to headquarters."

* * *

Craig Burke sat in his office and read the note that was included with the DVD. He then set it aside and watched the DVD. He suddenly had a clear understanding of the fear that Hector had of the girl. The video left no doubt as to Hector's role in the murder of Gabrielle. In addition to the earlier videos, a new video had been added. This one was of Roger Bentley lying in bed asleep alongside his dead wife with the bloody knife in his hand.

He printed out a still image of Roger lying beside Mimi and then locked the DVD in his office safe. A few minutes later he was handing the print to Jason Wood.

"What is it?" asked Jason Wood.

"Proof that Shannon Brewer killed Mimi Bentley," said Craig. "Proof that we can't use to clear Roger, but proof none the same."

The attorney stared at the print for several minutes before speaking again.

"Where did you get this?"

Craig explained the morning's events and then said, "And we can't use any of this."

"I want to see that whole DVD," said Jason Wood.

"I'm afraid I can't let you see that without first getting clearance from Roger Bentley and possibly one other person. I just thought you should see this image. It might pop up at the trial, or in the media, and you needed to know it might be out there. Also, your investigators seem to be getting off track. They need to focus on finding Shannon and not investigating me and my employees. I've got reports coming in that they're looking to pin this on me or some of the guards, and it wasn't one of us. They're just wasting time looking for anyone but her."

"They're looking at anyone and everyone to find a way to clear Roger. If that bothers you then too bad, you're not paying me, he is."

The lawyer was staring at the print and muttering to himself.

"I need to see that DVD," said Jason Wood.

"Then get me in to see Roger. If he approves, I'll let you see it."

"Let's go then," said the lawyer. "Let's see Roger and see what he says."

* * *

Shannon had positioned herself so that she could watch the men from Bentley Security leaving the hotel. She was pleased to see them looking frustrated as they left. She quickly made her way from the area and back to her nearby safe house. Once there she pondered her next move. If Craig Burke and his men obeyed her orders, then this could end quickly. She didn't expect that though. She now had one primary target left to get at. This one would be challenging. The Secret Service protection assigned to him guaranteed that she'd have her work cut out for her. The likelihood of her getting close enough to carry out an attack was minimal. This target would take time and effort to bring in. She smiled to herself. She loved a challenge.

* * *

Roger Bentley read the note handed him by Craig Burke and shook his head slowly.

"No way," muttered Roger. "She still has the video?"

"She left us a copy. It now includes a video of you and Mimi after her death."

"What else is on that video?" asked Jason Wood.

"I can't tell you that," said Roger. "You can't see it. Trust me, you don't want to know."

"She's getting bolder," said Craig. "I'm not sure if that's a good sign or not."

"Can we use this photo to exonerate me?" asked Roger.

"Not without some knowledge of who took it and when they took it," answered Jason. "It's a relatively low-resolution image and it would be pretty easy to argue that it was fabricated if we couldn't produce the person who took it. We'd need someone to verify the image."

"We've got to get our hands on that girl," said Roger.

"Believe me, we're trying," said Craig. "She's just not easy to catch."

"Why did she leave the video?" asked Jason.

"I have a feeling she'll tell us why when she's ready," said Craig.

"I need to have that DVD," said Jason. "I'd like to have it taken apart and find out who made it and when and where."

"We can't do that," muttered Roger. "My people will take a look at the information on it concerning authoring and creation, but even they aren't allowed to see the content. Even I haven't seen the content and I don't want to. Do you think she'll release it?"

"I don't know," answered Craig. "I doubt it. God knows she's had the opportunity to do so before now and she hasn't. I would have expected her to have released it after the death of her husband and son. When she didn't then, I wondered if she still had it. This proves she still has it."

"It's a valuable card for her," mused Roger. "If she plays it, then it's gone forever. She'll want to hold it as long as possible. The longer she holds the card, the more powerful the card becomes and therefore the more power she feels. We need to get to her. We need to get to her files and records and destroy that video while not damaging any information that can be used to exonerate me. Given what we know of her past, chances are pretty good that we could use some of the information she has for our purposes. We need those files."

"The question is how to find them?" reminded Craig. "The girl's not stupid. She has a plan and knows what she's doing. She set up that drop perfectly. She knew we provided security for the hotel. She even wore the same clothes and hairstyle that were in the photos she knew we had of her. She registered in her former name and even used one of her old credit cards. She's bold, resourceful, and damned smart. Catching her is next to impossible."

"You're going to have to tell Hector about this," said Roger. "He needs to know that this video is still out there. He needs to be prepared should it come out."

"I'll talk to him," said Craig.

* * *

The meetings between Craig and Hector were not so easy to arrange anymore. There were layers of people between the two men now and fighting his way through those layers took Craig several hours.

"I can only give you a few minutes," said Hector as Craig was finally shown into the Oval Office.

"It won't take more than a few minutes," said Craig. He paused while the doors to the room were closed. "Shannon Brewer is back and she's handed us a copy of the video."

"Damn! What does that mean?"

"I don't know. She's playing her own game and I don't know the rules. She was making a point of reminding us that she has the video. She's also now tacked on a video of Roger and Mimi lying side by side in bed with Mimi dead."

"So it was her," muttered Hector.

"That's not a real big surprise."

"I need that video."

"Roger wants our tech guys to take it apart and try to find out anything they can. I can maybe get you a copy of it, but the fewer copies there are out there the better it is for everyone. You should also take a look at your security. If she could get to Roger in his house, then she might be able to get to you."

Hector laughed and then waved his hand around the room.

"This building is the safest place in the world. She can't reach me here. There are nearly one hundred Secret Service agents in this place at any one time. She's good, but even she can't get past one hundred well-trained agents. She's not a physical threat to me. She's only a political threat. Now that I'm elected that threat becomes less worrisome, at least for now.

"I don't run another campaign for three more years. Even if the tape went public, without someone to vouch for it the tape is useless. There's no physical evidence to implicate me. Gabrielle's body has deteriorated to the point where it is useless as evidence. It would be bad publicity, but I can overcome that. I can even spin it in my favor. The other party can't use it without looking insensitive. It's a non-starter. Let her do what she wants, she can't hurt me."

* * *

Craig Burke awoke with every nerve on edge. Something was wrong. Surviving two wars and many dangerous encounters had heightened his senses to the point where he could immediately sense danger and he felt a danger unlike any he'd felt before. He went to move but found his arms and legs bound. As he struggled against the bonds, the light alongside his bed came on.

"Guess who?" asked Shannon Brewer playfully.

"Oh, shit!" muttered Craig.

"Nope! Try again."

"Shannon Brewer."

"Bingo!"

"Are you here to kill me?" asked Craig noticing the IV in his left arm.

"Not unless I have to. I want to have a chat. The IV was started so I could counter the drug I used to knock you out. It also comes in handy if I need to knock you back out again."

"Why are you here?"

"I thought I'd drop by and say hi. See how you're doing. See how you liked the DVD."

"I've seen better videos. Why did you drop that off?"

"I thought it might help things a bit. How did you like the video of your boss and his wife?"

"I thought it was a tad gruesome. It seemed unlike you. You normally make clean kills. I also thought you only targeted those who were going to die anyway?"

"Mimi had advanced cancer. She wasn't telling anyone. She'd just found out herself a couple of days before. She had just a few months of life at most and those months would likely be pretty unpleasant."

"What? How did you know that?"

"I followed her to her doctor's office. I was lurking outside the window when she got the news. She took it well. The lady was a rock. She knew something was seriously wrong. The doc advised her that no treatment option existed and that all he could do was help her cope with the pain. Check the autopsy results and you'll see they confirm what I say. She was already in a lot of pain and taking meds to help cope. Things were going to get a lot worse for her. She was also building up a stockpile of drugs to take herself out when things got too bad. I just ended her suffering. She was unconscious when she was killed. She felt nothing. It was a bit messier than normal for me, but I needed it messy to send the message to your boss."

"Cancer? I didn't know."

"It happens," said Shannon casually. "She was conflicted on taking her own life, but the pain was already making her think about it. I just put her out of her misery."

"By murdering her."

"I drugged her to the point where she felt nothing. If you have an animal that's suffering and you don't put them down you can get charged with animal cruelty. I don't see the difference. Life is life. Let's get back to the DVD. The video I included of Roger and Mimi lying alongside each other in bed proves that I was there. I have more proof of my presence that could get your boss acquitted."

"And your price is?"

"See, I knew you were a smart man. The price is one hundred million dollars."

"There is no way! He won't part with that kind of money. His lawyer will get him acquitted. We can work with the jury to get an acquittal for much less. All we need is one juror and it's not that hard to swing one juror. It would cost a hell of a lot less to buy a juror."

"Getting acquitted is one thing. I'm talking about his life. What's that worth to him? He has to go back and forth to the courthouse for the trial. It's easy to pick him off at any number of places along the route. The same is true of his life in prison. The yard where he's forced to go for exercise once a day is pretty exposed.

Take a look around the next time you're there. The place is designed to keep prisoners in, but that fencing wouldn't stop a sniper from eliminating a prisoner. No matter how hard you try, you can't protect him while he's in custody. I can kill him anytime I want to. If he pays me what I want, then he lives. If he doesn't, then he dies. It's that simple."

"One hundred million dollars is a lot of money He won't have that readily available."

"He has over forty million in a Swiss bank account. He has another thirty million in each of two Caribbean banks. There's another seventy-some million spread out through banks around the world. All of it stashed in numbered accounts accessible to him. He could give me one hundred million in a matter of minutes without attracting any undue attention. I did my homework."

"I'll take it to him and see what he says. He's going to want to know about the proof and any other conditions."

"The only other condition is that you guys leave me alone. If I find anyone hunting me ever again, then the deal is off and I'll come hunting and I won't settle for less than the head of everyone involved. As for the proof, suffice to say I'll supply the camera that was used to take the video of Roger and Mimi. There are some other videos on that memory card that would work to exonerate Roger. I've also uploaded the videos to a third-party site that will have timestamps showing when the videos were uploaded should there be a timing issue raised in court."

"Can I get a preview of those videos?"

"Sorry, no."

"I have to take you at your word?"

"What other choice do you have?"

"There's been some talk of using those close to you to motivate you to cooperate."

"You've already killed everyone who was truly close to me."

"What about the Underwoods?"

"You don't want to go messing with them," said Shannon with a laugh. "Have you met Celia Underwood?"

"Not personally," said Craig. "But, she went out west nosing around about you. I just learned about that recently and we're still evaluating how to handle that."

"You don't mess with Celia if you know what's good for you. I tend to be cautious. I tend to plot and plan. Celia is a force of nature. She reacts. If you harm Tommy or her kids, she'll track you down and kill you. There won't be any subtlety either. She'll drive a truck through your front door. That's not the girl to mess with. I've seen her mad and you don't want to go there. Your security guards wouldn't stop her. Nothing would stop her."

"I've known a few women like that."

"Not like Celia. She's a force of nature when aroused. I was surprised Tommy let you guys go. I thought he just might hold you forever."

"He wanted to, but he came under some pretty intense political pressure. While I was with him he got calls from the Governor and a couple of Senators. He still wouldn't let us go, though. He almost seemed more determined to keep holding us with each call. It was only when the evidence came back exonerating us that he had to relent. It was stupid on his part. It cost him his political future. The party's going to back the prosecutor for the Sheriff's job and they've taken away his party membership."

"That won't stop Tommy if he still wants the job. You said they'd picked the prosecutor for sheriff? That's stupid. Celia knows him. She grew up with him. Whatever skeletons he has hidden in his closet; Celia will find them and bring them out. That was a dumb move on the party's part. They should have brought in someone who wasn't known to Celia. She's not someone they want to cross."

"I was wondering why he put her in charge of his campaign."

"She wouldn't have given him any choice. You don't mess with Celia. Those guards of yours wouldn't stand a chance of stopping her."

"Where is my security detail?" asked Craig.

"They're drugged, but alive. Don't worry about them. They'll wake up around the time the next shift comes along. They'll be fine. You might want to have a chat with them about not all buying coffee from the same pot at the same convenience store. It just makes it too easy to take them out. I simply drugged one pot of coffee before they came in and then emptied it afterward. That's a lesson you should learn too. By the way, how many men do you have patrolling your perimeter?"

"Four."

"That's what I thought you'd say. What would you say if I told you there were five? There are four looking out and one looking in?"

"I'd say you were wrong."

Shannon smiled and reached into her bag and removed some items that she dropped on the bedside table.

"What's that?"

"Wallet, gun, and some papers from the fifth man," said Shannon. "I suspect the identity papers were forged. It's a good job, though. This guy's a pro. He moves like a ghost. So does his partner. They take twelve-hour shifts watching you. It looks like you have another enemy. I thought you might like to know about them."

"What do you want? This isn't about money is it?"

"I want my husband and son back. I want my old life back. But, you can't do that. No one can do that."

"We weren't trying to kill anyone."

"Sure," replied Shannon sarcastically. "That was an ambush. You weren't going to leave any of us alive. I suspect the plan wasn't to kill me immediately. You would have used the safety of my husband and son as leverage to get the information you wanted from me before you killed all three of us. You knew I wouldn't let them suffer. I'm not stupid. You wouldn't leave any survivors. You guys aren't that sloppy. If all you wanted to do was kill me, then a sniper could have picked me off easily. You had men there. I've seen the photos. It would have been easy to pick me off then, but you didn't."

"Snipers can miss. We didn't want to take the chance on just wounding you and having you hunting us."

"Like I am now," mused Shannon.

"How is your shoulder?"

"It's good enough. It gets a bit cranky first thing in the morning, but it's usable."

"How the hell did you make that climb at Roger's house with a bad shoulder? I almost killed myself doing that."

"I've done harder things. Besides, I'm a tad lighter than you are. I was also more highly motivated. You were stupid in doing it hand over hand. That just makes it harder. Use your legs the next time. Wrap them around the wire with a plastic skid plate under your calves and the trip is a ton easier."

"You were watching me?"

"I've been watching everything. Did you think I'd let you guys kill my husband and son and destroy everything I own without coming back? And why did you burn down that house? I loved that house. Did you think I'd be stupid enough to have the video at my house?"

"It seemed like a good idea at the time. Besides, even if you didn't have the video there, you might have left a clue behind to the location. We needed that video."

"Did you ever consider just contacting me to try and buy it?"

Craig snorted and replied, "Yeah. That's a good idea. I'm sure you wouldn't have another copy of it hidden somewhere. The only way to be sure that the video was stopped was by taking out everyone who did or might know of it and hopefully destroying the video in the process. We failed in that mission."

"You might find this hard to believe, but my word is good. If I give my word that the video won't come out, then it won't come out. I've never released one yet and I've been given reason to on a couple of occasions. Just ask Hector about that. He sent people after me once before. I gave him a pass that time. I'm getting a lot less forgiving now."

"We can't have anyone in a position where they can blackmail the President."

"You should have thought of that before you guys nominated a guy with a closet full of skeletons. Now about that hundred million dollars…"

"What do we get for the hundred million?"

"Everyone lives. The video stays in my private collection and doesn't get seen. I'll also promise not to blackmail the President if that makes you guys feel any better."

"I'm not sure we can agree with that."

"It'll be safer for the lot of you if you did. There isn't a lot of safety with me running around loose. Roger's going to be running back and forth to that courthouse for his trial. It's child's play to take him out. Even the prison yard is an open and easy place to make a kill. Roger Bentley's life is mine to take any time I want. The same is true of Hector's. He thinks he's safe with his Secret Service protection and living in the White House, but he's not. I can reach him anytime I want to. As for you, I think you'll agree that your current position makes you aware of your vulnerability. One hundred million dollars for me to go away and let you all live seems like a bargain to me."

"It won't to them. Not as long as you still have that video."

"Can you get in contact with Roger?"

"When I have to get in touch I can. I've met with him before. I can get access again if I have to."

"Get in touch with him tomorrow. Tell him the terms I've set down. You also might want to alert him that I'll be sending Hector a message shortly. It will be a very clear message."

"How do we get in touch with you?"

"That's easy. If you guys agree to my terms, then simply come out and strongly endorse Tommy Underwood in his run for Sheriff. That means the Governor, Senators, and President. When I see those guys standing by Tommy and endorsing him, then I'll know you agree and make contact. If I don't see that, then I go hunting for real and all of you guys die. As for you, it's time you went back to sleep."

She leaned forward and injected a white liquid into his IV. Craig felt everything get warm and fuzzy and then he was gone.

* * *

Craig awoke the following morning and groaned. He was pleased to see that his arms and legs were no longer bound, but he was angry that Shannon had been able to penetrate his security perimeter. He picked up the papers she'd left behind from the fifth man and then left the room. He used his cellular phone to call in some reinforcements. A few minutes later a line of his security men was arrayed in a circle around his house and grounds and the search was on for the mystery man that Shannon had reported. The man was found with his arms cuffed around a tree. He was cut free and then brought into the house for questioning.

"Who are you?" asked Craig as the man sat bound in a chair facing him.

"You already know that. You've got my wallet. How did you get that?"

"It was a gift. The woman who gave it to me thought the identity papers had been forged. That would mean you aren't who these papers say you are. Now, who are you?"

"I don't know what you're talking about. I was just out walking in the woods and woke up to find myself cuffed to a tree. I have no idea what happened."

Craig excused the rest of the men from the room and then turned to confront the man.

"I don't know who you are, and truth be told, I don't care. I'm assuming you're not here to kill me. So, why are you watching me?"

"I'm not."

"Don't make this any harder than it has to be. Shannon told me you'd been out there for several days and were taking shifts with another watcher. I know you've been watching me. What I don't know is why."

"Shannon? Who is Shannon?"

"Shannon Brewer. She's the woman who drugged you last night and brought me your papers. Don't be overly concerned, she drugged me and my men also. Why were you watching me?"

"I wasn't drugged," said the man confusedly.

"Morning came fast today, didn't it? How do you suppose I got your papers? How did you end up handcuffed to a tree? You were drugged. We all were. She got us with the coffee at a convenience store. Did you get coffee there last night?"

"Yeah," said the man. "What the hell is going on? Who is this Shannon Brewer?"

"Welcome to my world. More important right now is who are you?"

"I'm a private investigator. I was hired by the lawyers representing Roger Bentley."

"You're watching the wrong man," said Craig untying the man. "I had nothing to do with the death of Mimi. You want Shannon Brewer, not me."

"How do I find her?"

"Damned if I know. If I knew that, I'd have her, but I don't. Now I'm nothing more than a messenger boy for her."

"You're a messenger boy?"

"Yes, I've got to take a message to Roger Bentley from her today. That's what all of this was about last night. You're coming with me to Jason Wood's office.

Once he vouches for you, you'll be free to go. If he doesn't, then things might get a tad more intense for you."

* * *

Roger Bentley was not happy with the choice offered to him.

"One hundred million dollars?" asked Roger incredulously. "Is she insane?"

"It could be. She's also damned dangerous."

"How much danger am I in?"

"Look around you. There are lots of woods around this prison that make it easy to set up a sniper's perch. She could pick you off pretty easily. I know her capabilities. It's well within her capabilities. The same is true for the transport back and forth to the courthouse. Those trips are arranged to prevent escape, not assassination. There are a limited number of routes to and from the courthouse. If she wants you dead, then you'll be dead."

"And she swears she'll get me out of this in exchange for the money?"

"That's what she said. If she has what she says, then it's probably enough to at least, establish reasonable doubt."

"And she won't be hunting me anymore?"

"That's what she said, though I'm not sure I believe her."

"Why don't you believe her?"

"She has plenty of money. Based on our latest estimates we believe she has more than fifty million dollars stashed away. She can live pretty comfortably on that. She wants vengeance. At least she did. I don't think she'll just walk away. I think she's trying to get you to give her the money she wants and then she'll kill you, or more likely leave you at the mercy of the justice system."

"So, what do we do?"

"That's your call. She wants a hell of a lot of money and there's no guarantee she'll deliver what she says she will. My instincts are that she won't deliver. I don't think she wants to see you go free. If I was her, I'd take the money and either let you rot in jail, or kill you. She'll likely want the money before she'll give us the proof we need. Once she has the money, I'm thinking she'll just disappear and either kill you or leave you here."

"I don't trust her."

"We might have another option." Craig then explained his plan.

"Hector won't like it."

"She said she'd be sending him a message in the next couple of days. Maybe that will influence his opinion."

* * *

"Another boring day," muttered Montgomery Cramer, lead sniper of one of the six counter-sniper teams positioned on the roof of the White House.

"I like boring," said Carrie Groves, his spotter. "It beats the hell out of the alternative."

Montgomery, Monty to nearly everyone, simply shrugged and resumed his surveillance. Both were examining the buildings in their sector that overlooked the White House Oval Office. Every roof and window of every building within the sniper's range facing the White House was examined on a routine basis. Each sniper team had a series of buildings assigned to them. The protocol called for a search from the nearest building to the farthest. The area closest to the White House would be examined first, assuming that the largest threat would come from a close-in threat.

Once those areas were cleared, the surveillance would then move to the closest building. The examination would begin with the roof and work its way down the building floor by floor, window by window until the entire building had been examined. Any discrepancy would be noted and checked. An open window where it was normally closed would draw their attention and be investigated by one of the ground units. Until they were able to give a reason for the open window, one of the sniper teams would be trained on that window ready to take out an enemy sniper.

Any discrepancy on the rooftops would be checked out by one of the three air units that were on standby around the city. Anyone moving on a rooftop within a certain range of the White House could be assured of being in the sights of at least one sniper the whole time they were exposed. Even activity behind closed windows that seemed suspicious would attract the attention of the sniper team. These men and women spent eight hours a day staring out at the buildings around them and they knew the comings and goings of everyone in the area better than even the best doorman. They not only saw people coming and going, but they had high-powered views of the interior of each room. They knew who was having an affair, who used drugs, and who slept on the job. Nothing escaped their attention.

"Hey, Monty," said Carrie. "Did you see the new drapes in apartment 3C of building four?"

"Yeah," said Montgomery. "They've been fixing the place up. Not sure I agree with their taste in paint color though."

"It is kind of ugly," agreed Carrie. "Do we report the drapes?"

"Yeah," said Monty. Eighteen years of military sniping and then the promotion to the White House where he'd rapidly climbed to the top, and now he was spending his time noting the window treatments in apartments. While it was theoretically important to note any change that could help hide a sniper, in practice, it was not likely that any sniper would attempt an attack on the White House. The risk was even more remote on a day like today when there were no outside activities scheduled. The President was to be in the Oval Office all day and that was among the most heavily shielded rooms in the building. The odds of anyone attempting anything were extremely remote, but his job was to note any changes and by God, he would. He took that job seriously as his current position was directly above the Oval Office and his field of view involved the buildings that offered a glimpse into the office.

* * *

Hector had spent most of the morning sitting at his desk in the oval office reading various briefing papers. The boredom was killing him and he got up to stretch his legs. As he moved away from the desk he heard a sound behind him. A cloud of smoke was rising from behind his desk and he saw a hole in the window behind where he'd been sitting.

"What the hell?" muttered Hector. He took half a step towards the desk when the Secret Service agents raced into the room and grabbed him.

"Go! Go! Go!" screamed the lead agent to the agents on either side of Hector who had grabbed him by the arms and they were sprinting towards the door leading from the Oval Office. Hector saw the world go by him in a blur as he was half carried, half dragged through the offices towards the bunker in the basement of the White House.

* * *

Montgomery had just finished his sweep of the last building and lowered his rifle when he heard it. At first, he wasn't sure what he'd heard, but then it quickly sank in that there had been an unusual sound from the area below him. That was followed a second later by the report from a distant rifle. The radio chatter indicated that something had happened in the Oval Office and that was all Monty and his partner needed to hear. They were quickly scanning the surrounding buildings looking for a target, but nothing presented itself.

A second sniper team came over to assist, but the four pairs of eyes were unable to find anything suspicious. The radio was crackling in their ears with reports of an attack on the Oval Office. It was quickly confirmed that the President was alive and unhurt and being escorted to the bunker in the sub-basement of the White

House. What had caused the damage to the Oval Office was not so clear. The first report that the window of the Oval Office had been penetrated shocked Monty. While nothing was truly bulletproof, that glass was as bullet-resistant as anything in the world. For a bullet to penetrate it was nearly unthinkable. His team redoubled their efforts to find the source, but once again came up empty.

"That seemed like a long delay between the impact and the sound of the shot," muttered Monty.

"I thought so too," said Carrie. "Two shots maybe?"

"What does the shot tracing computer say?" asked Monty nodding to a nearby computer terminal. Connected to the computer was a series of microphones placed around the roof of the White House that tracked every noise and sound. Every sound was digitized and identified by the computer. Most sounds were ignored, but anything that could be an explosion or gunshot was highlighted. The system could theoretically determine exactly where the shot came from by comparing the time it took for the sounds of the shot to arrive at each microphone. In practice, the system had proven so unreliable that it was seldom relied upon.

Carrie flipped up the display and quickly scanned the results.

"You're not going to like it," said Carrie.

"What is it?"

"The computer says the shot came from two miles away to the Southeast on bearing 223 degrees."

"Two miles? Hand me the spotting scope."

Carrie handed him the higher-powered spotting scope and held Monty's rifle while he scanned the buildings farther out.

"Son of a bitch!" muttered Monty.

"Find something?" asked Carrie.

"It looks like it," said Monty. "Get the ground units moving. There's something there."

* * *

"What the hell was that?" asked Hector with a note of disbelief as the Secret Service agents escorted his wife into the bunker.

"We don't know yet, Sir," said the agent who was escorting his wife. "Something penetrated the window. We're still looking for the source. We should have something pinned down pretty soon."

"Was it a bullet?" asked Carol.

"Yes, Ma'am," said her agent. "We think it was, but we're still looking into it. We'll know more soon."

"I thought the White House was bulletproof?"

"It's bullet-resistant," said her agent. "We can't make it completely safe, but it's as safe as we can make it. After this, we'll reevaluate conditions and make improvements to prevent this from happening again."

"How long do we have to stay down here?" asked Hector.

"It'll be a while," said the agent. "We have to be sure that the threat is eliminated before we can let you back above ground."

"How long?" asked Hector.

"It will probably be the rest of the day."

"That's unacceptable! I can't be seen cowering in the basement of the White House. What about moving us to Camp David?"

"You don't understand the significance of this threat," said the agent patiently. "That slug can penetrate any shield we have. It can destroy your motorcade. It can bring down the helicopter. It could bring down Air Force One. It could take out a tank. This is a big weapon and we can't take any chances. It has a long range and is very dangerous. We now believe the shot was fired from about two miles away and still had enough power to penetrate the Oval Office. That's a serious weapon."

"What about our children?" asked Carol Esteban.

"We've got them and they're on their way to a safe location. They'll be fine. We'll bring them here once we know the building is secure."

"Are we safe here?" asked Carol Esteban.

"This shelter would protect you from a nuclear blast. You're safe here."

"But, we can't leave?"

"Not until we evaluate this threat and find a way to counter it."

* * *

"What do you see?" asked Carrie.

"Use the spotting scope," said Montgomery. "Look at the red brick building to the southeast. There's an open window on the seventh floor. Look at the table inside the window."

Carrie zoomed in on the plywood table that was sitting in the middle of the space. Atop the table was a long cylindrical object sitting upright. Next to that was a folded piece of cardboard with writing on it. In large black letters, someone had written "Bang!"

"Send a ground team there," said Montgomery still examining the area. There was a small black object on the table also, but he couldn't tell what it was.

"Does that look like a shell casing to you?" asked Carrie.

"It could be," said Montgomery referring to the upright cylindrical object. "It's a cute note. Someone's trying to send us a message."

"That's over two miles away," said Carrie. "How do we stop that?"

"We need to figure that out and we need to do so quickly."

Monty kept up surveillance of the seventh-floor area until the first ground team arrived and reported the area secure. He then resumed monitoring the surrounding areas in hope of finding something on which to vent the frustration he was starting to feel welling up in him.

* * *

The first Secret Service unit to arrive at the site of the shooting secured the area and waited for the FBI to arrive to collect any evidence that might exist. Within minutes that part of the city was swarming with Federal agents from nearly every investigative branch of the government. Throughout the rest of the city, chaos was reigning. All roads into and out of the city had been closed as soon as word of the shooting had been reported. Vehicles attempting to leave the city were searched. The airports had been shut down along with the bus lines, train lines, and any other means for a person to escape the city. Every route out of the city was blocked and the city was shut down. Every federal building was locked down with those inside forced to remain there. Subways were stopped and no one was allowed to leave the train. Teams of investigators roamed the city checking out known threats in the hope of finding the person responsible. The city was stopped dead and chaos was taking over.

The FBI was followed to the shooting site by hordes of media and soon the world was watching as the FBI investigators entered and left the building. Neighbors were interviewed and soon a profile of an Arabic-looking man carrying a large package was circulating. It didn't take long for the commentators to brand this a terror attack carried out by Middle Eastern extremists. It also wasn't long before the first reprisal took place against a mosque in a Washington suburb.

Among the items removed from the scene of the shooting was a memory card containing a video. The FBI viewed the video and had copies of it available for the Secret Service. Montgomery and Carrie were called down to see the video. The two were now seated in front of a video monitor watching the feed.

"The shooter was using a sight with a video camera built-in," said the lead Secret Service investigator. "They left this as a calling card." He hit play and then stood back.

For the next twenty minutes, the three watched as the video played out. The first image was of the Esteban children leaving the White House on their way to school. Seeing the kids in the crosshairs of a rifle scope was unnerving. The video briefly blacked out only to come back with the children in their school. The sniper focused the sight on the older child and then the younger one as they sat at their desks in the classroom. Both children were in the crosshairs for several minutes.

Then the screen went black again and came back as the scope was zooming in on the White House. The image came into focus as the scope focused on the upper floors of the White House. For eight minutes, the scope tracked Carol Esteban as she sat at a table and then moved around the spaces.

"Why didn't he shoot?" asked Carrie.

"This is just a message tape," said Monty. "The shooter is showing us what he can do. He's giving us a warning of what he's capable of."

This was soon shown to be true as the shooter then moved the sight down to the Oval Office. For the next ten minutes, the scope remained focused on the head of the President of the United States as he sat in his desk chair. The three agents charged with protecting him felt uncomfortable with what they saw. It was only when the President rose from his chair and moved away from the desk that the scope moved from his head and focused on the back of the chair. The image shook slightly as the shot was fired and then briefly refocused on the room as the Secret Service agents rushed in and removed the President.

"That's an amazing shot from that range," muttered Montgomery appreciatively.

"It's pretty impressive," agreed Carrie.

"He hit within an inch or two of where he was aiming. At that range, that's amazing. Add in the deflections from going through the glass and any obstacles along the way and that's remarkable. Just the wind and air currents on a shot of over a mile can easily move it a foot or more. That was a hell of a shot."

"It missed the President," pointed out Carrie.

"Whoever the shooter was, he wasn't trying to hit the President or Mrs. Esteban," said Montgomery. "This was a message shot. Whoever did this was sending a message to somebody."

"Us?" asked Carrie.

"They were sending it to somebody, us, the President, his wife, the country, someone. Is there anything else on the video? Are there any other messages?"

"Nothing that we've found yet," said the other Secret Service agent. "How do we defend against this type of threat?"

"It's not going to be easy," said Montgomery. "Even if we saw the shooter, we couldn't intervene at that range. Our weapons just don't have that kind of range. Even if they did, using rifles with that kind of firepower in a city, shooting out at soft targets would likely result in significant collateral damage. A slug with that kind of power would pass right through the target and probably through most walls.

Anything we could develop to counter that kind of weapon would be nearly too powerful to use.

"Unless our shooter was nice enough to stand in front of some armor, we'd only be able to respond in the most extreme circumstances. If we saw him before the shot, we'd have to send a ground unit over to intervene. We could use lasers or some other means to temporarily blind the shooter, but we couldn't shoot them from that range. Lasers to blind the shooter might be our best option."

"What about stationing more snipers partway out?" asked the other agent. "That would get them close enough to the target to act."

"Line of fire is the problem," said Montgomery. "The reason we stay on the roof of the building is that we can use pretty much the same line of fire as the shooter. Being more than a few feet out of the line of fire can blind our snipers if we put them on adjacent buildings. You need to be in the same line of sight to ensure an ability to act. If our guys were too high, too low, or off to one side or the other, they'd be useless. No, all we can do is hope to detect them before they can get a shot off and intervene quickly using ground forces at that range."

"We can step up the ground patrols in the suspect areas," said the other agent.

"We'll need more eyes also," said Montgomery. "As it is now, it takes us nearly fifteen minutes to make a sweep of our existing responsibilities. If we expand that radius out to where this shooting originated, then we're looking at needing to at least double the number of eyes available. Given the penetration of the slug, it might make sense to move it out even further than that. That's especially true for outdoor events. That slug penetrated deeply through a hell of a lot of stuff. If all you were looking to do is kill an unprotected person, you could probably increase the range."

* * *

Hector was pacing back and forth in the bunker for several minutes waiting for an update from the Secret Service. When it came he wasn't happy.

"What do you mean you can't guarantee the safety of my family and me?" demanded Hector Esteban. "That's your job!"

"This type of weapon presents unique challenges to us, Sir," said the head of the Secret Service. "The slug, in this case, was a depleted uranium slug that had been coated with some sort of coating to enhance its penetration ability. The density of the slug and the coating when combined with the velocity of it is nearly unstoppable. At a range under a mile, such a combination would penetrate at least ten inches of our heaviest armor.

"The shooter, in this case, was over two miles away and was still able to penetrate our defenses. We can't add enough protection to fully shield anyone from such a weapon. In an exposed location, that slug would easily go through anything we could put around you. None of our vehicles can withstand such a weapon. The shooter can pretty much destroy anything we put you in, other than the bunker. We're looking at our options to enhance the security. Right now we're looking more to obscuring the view and adding some additional protection. We've got some concrete barriers coming to shield the Oval Office and we're looking at various materials to make it impossible for someone outside to see inside the structure. As we get sections of the facility updated we'll let you move into those sections, but we've got to act prudently until this threat is neutralized."

"I can't govern from here," muttered Hector. "Who did this? Who tried to kill me?"

"We're fairly confident that the person behind this wasn't trying to kill you, Sir. There was a video recovered from the scene that showed that the sniper had your children, you, and Mrs. Esteban in his sight for an extended time. In total, all of you were in the cross-hairs for nearly twenty minutes. Had the shooter intended you harm, you'd most likely be dead now. We feel that this was a message shot. Someone was trying to communicate something, but we don't know what. They were telling us you were vulnerable, but why?"

Hector felt the blood flush from his body and he collapsed into a chair.

"Are you okay, Sir?"

"Get me Craig Burke!" said Hector.

"Sir," said the head of the Secret Service. "We're in lockdown mode right now. No one should be brought in here until this situation is resolved. I can assure you that Bentley Security can do nothing against this type of threat."

"Get him here!" demanded Hector. "Now!"

"Yes, Sir."

It was nearly an hour later when Craig Burke was shown into the bunker.

"I always wondered what this place looked like," said Craig as Hector showed him to a chair.

"Was it her?" asked Hector.

"Probably. She said she'd send a message. This sure looks like a message shot if you can believe the press reports."

"They said she had me in her sights for ten minutes before she shot," said Hector shakily. "They're saying she could have killed me anytime she wanted to. I thought I was safe here."

"No one's safe as long as that girl is running around and hunting us. We screwed up when we went after her and didn't get her. We've made her more dangerous than she was before and she was plenty dangerous to start with."

"What do we do?"

"We don't have a lot of options. She claims she'll drop everything in exchange for one hundred million dollars, but neither Roger nor I believe that to be true. She should have enough money already. She wants blood, his first probably and then yours. I'm probably on her hit list also."

"So, what do we do?"

"We have to get Roger someplace safe. He's a sitting duck where he is now. We've got his place in the Caribbean updated and it should be safe from her unless she has a nuke someplace that we don't know about. The way things are going I'm not sure I'd rule that out. The service will do as good a job of protecting you as they can. What we need to do is get everyone someplace safe and then lure her out into the open."

"And how do we do that?"

"We need bait. We need to hold something she feels strongly enough about to take a chance to come out into the open and then we can get her."

"What do we use for bait though?"

"I'm thinking the Underwoods," said Craig.

"Who are they?"

"They're friends of hers from Virginia. She's the godparent to their young children. She was best friends with Celia Underwood. She called Tommy Underwood to tell him where my men were after she'd killed them. She has ties to them. If we take them and hold them she'll likely try to save them. It may be our best option."

"The sheriff?" asked Hector finally putting the names together.

"Yes."

"You've got to be kidding me? You want to kidnap a sheriff?"

"We need something for bait and she still has ties to them. She wants you to publicly endorse Tommy Underwood for sheriff as proof that we agree to her terms. Not just you, but the governor, senators, and others also. She still has ties to them. It's about the only card we have left to play."

"We just got done politically isolating him and now we're supposed to endorse him?"

"That's what she wants."

"So, she still has ties to the Underwoods?"

"It looks that way."

"How will this work?"

"I'm not sure you want to know all of the details. It's probably better for you if you can deny knowing anything about this."

"I need to know what's going to happen," insisted Hector.

"We can grab the Underwoods and hold them at one of our facilities. We can notify her through her old e-mail address that we'll exchange them for the videos and her promised silence. We'll give her a deadline in which to comply."

"And she'll just go along with that?"

"Not likely. I suspect she'll try to rescue them. I'm counting on it. You should be safe here, but Roger is somewhat exposed. We'll either have to find a way to protect him or get him out of the area. If we can keep both of you guys safe then she'll come after me, or try to rescue the Underwoods. I'm thinking she'll try to save them. We'll have a few surprises waiting for her. It'll look like they're being held by a relatively small group and she's ballsy enough that she'll think she can get them out. We'll have a substantially larger force lying in wait for her however and we'll catch her."

"Then what happens? Do you think you can make her talk? Can you get a confession out of her?"

"If we can get our hands on her then we can get the information we need, but we have to get her first. She's already told me she'd have given up the tape to prevent her husband and child from suffering. I'm pretty sure she'll do the same for the Underwoods."

"Okay," said Hector. "Let's end this thing."

CHAPTER EIGHT

Celia Underwood was watching her kids play out in the backyard when her phone rang. She picked up the phone and then slammed it down after no one said anything on the other end. That had happened twice earlier and she was getting tired of it. She turned to look back out at the kids and was annoyed that they weren't in her immediate view. She opened the back door and walked outside to look for them when she felt something strike her in the side and then her body convulsed and everything went black.

* * *

Tommy Underwood had gone out to the Robinson place in response to old George Robinson's call about vandalism. He'd known old George for years and rather than send a deputy out on the call he'd taken it himself. George didn't respond well to 'them youngsters' as he called the deputies and always insisted on talking to the sheriff himself.

As Tommy parked his car and got out, he glanced around and saw the graffiti sprayed on the side of George's barn. As he walked over to examine it he sensed movement nearby and reached for his holster, but he was too slow. Something struck him in the side and he collapsed on the ground before losing consciousness.

* * *

Celia Underwood didn't know what had happened. She awoke blindfolded, gagged, and with her arms and legs bound. It was obvious she was in a vehicle of some sort from the movement, but she didn't know anything more than that. Panic set in at once over what was going to happen to her and what had happened to her kids. She tried calling out to them and could hear distant sobbing sounds coming from elsewhere in the vehicle.

She attempted to communicate through her gag and she was pretty sure her kids were there with her. She fought desperately against her restraints, but there was no give. When the vehicle had finally come to a stop she'd feared the worse and was surprised to hear something else be dropped on the floor near her before the vehicle door slammed shut and they took off again.

* * *

When Tommy regained consciousness he was blindfolded, gagged, and bound in the back of a vehicle of some sort bouncing along a road. He tried to work the blindfold off his eyes, but it was secured in such a way that there was no give. His arms and legs were securely tied together. As he struggled against his bonds he rubbed up against something and heard a muffled yell. He knew in an instant whose yell that was. No gag could disguise his wife's fury. Tommy edged his body over towards her and tried to grunt to communicate with her but there was little to be accomplished.

The vehicle seemed to drive on forever and then finally, the vehicle started bouncing down a very rough road throwing the bound occupants in the back against one another as it slowly bounced down the road. Finally, it stopped and they could hear the back door opening. One by one they were flung over the shoulder of someone and carried inside a structure.

Celia Underwood was the first to have her blindfold and gag removed. She frantically examined her children who were laying there and then her husband. All looked to be intact and undamaged.

"Who are you?" screamed Celia to the men standing guard over them. "Why are you doing this?"

They simply stared back impassively.

"Why are we here?"

Once again there was no response. One of the men picked up her from the floor and carried her across the floor to what looked like a prison cell with the door open. He carried her inside and then set her on a bench there while two others dragged her children across and dropped them inside. One more man then dragged her husband across the floor and dropped him there. Once all four Underwood's were within the cell and the cell door closed and locked, the man who had carried Celia in reached through the bars and grabbed the ropes binding her wrists. She winced as he pulled against them and then watched as he pulled a knife and sliced her wrists free and released her.

"You can untie them," said one of the men nodding towards her family as he checked that the door was secured. "There are water bottles and some food over there and there's a toilet in the corner. There are some clean clothes in those bags. You've got sleeping bags in the corner. Make yourselves comfortable. You'll be here a while."

"Why are we here?" asked Celia. "Who are you?"

The men simply turned and walked from the room. Celia removed the gags and blindfolds from everyone and then untied her husband's hands so the two of them could remove the ropes that bound their children. Once they were all finally untied Celia and Tommy spent some time calming the kids down and then examined their situation.

The cell was very well built and looked quite new. Tommy had little doubt that it had been built for them. The clothes had been purchased for them as everything was the correct size. He examined the materials within reach to try and devise some sort of weapon, but there was little available. His gun belt and pocket knife had been taken. There were sleeping bags for each of them, but no beds.

"Why are they doing this?" asked her daughter Grace. "Why are they locking us up?"

"This isn't about us," said Tommy Underwood after looking at his wife. "This is about Shannon. I think we're the bait they're using to lure her out of hiding."

"Do they think she's that stupid?" asked Celia.

* * *

The story of the disappearance of the Underwood family made national headlines. While most of the country pondered the meaning of the disappearance, one person had no doubt what it meant. Shannon Brewer glared at the screen for a few seconds after the initial announcement and knew that this was a message for her. She switched off the television and pondered the situation.

She knew that this was a trap. She wasn't stupid. She knew that the smart thing to do was to walk away, to abandon the Underwood family to their fate. She also knew that she couldn't live with herself if she did that. Shannon paced the room for quite some time pondering the possibilities. It was immediately obvious that Bentley Security was behind the kidnapping. But where would they have taken them? They were hoping to trap Shannon, but to trap her they had to lure her someplace. Where? Where would they take the Underwood's knowing that Shannon could find them?

Shannon pondered that possibility for some time and came up with several options. The Bentley mansion was secure, but Roger Bentley wouldn't want his fingerprints on this operation if things went badly. Craig Burke's house was too exposed. The corporate headquarters were also too well known with too many people coming and going. Where would Bentley Security hide four people securely without any fear of them being discovered? They controlled many prisons but the arrival of a woman and two children would be noticed. So where were they being held?

She spent several hours looking into possibilities before running out of ideas. As much as she hated to say it, Shannon needed some help. She bought a cheap disposable cellular phone and made a call.

"It's about time you called," said Charlie. "I was beginning to think you'd forgotten about me."

"You said I could call you if I needed help at any time," said Shannon. "I might need some help now. Have you heard about the Underwood's?"

"You don't need help. You need an army to get to them."

"Do you know where they are?"

"Of course, as soon as word broke I had people nosing around. I know where they are and all of the details you'll need to get them. I've got the help you'll need already in place. They have all of the maps, satellite photos, and details you'll need. Can you get to Richmond fairly easily?"

"What's in Richmond?"

"Your friends are being held in an old Bentley Security training facility near there. I've got some help on the ground for you there. They're waiting for you. There's a park in the center of town called Monroe Park. You'll find one of my guys walking Marley in the park every even hour. Marley's there to verify who you are to them and to verify that they're there on my behalf. The team leader will brief you on what we've found and provide you with any assistance you might need. Don't be afraid to use the tools I'm putting at your disposal. Those men are one hundred percent loyal."

"I owe you," said Shannon.

"No, you don't. But, these are bad guys and you'll need some help. If you want to keep the Underwoods alive, then you're going to need the help I'm making available."

"You're sure they're alive now?"

"They are for now. There's a time limit though. They won't hold them forever and they sure as hell won't let them go after this. If you don't take the bait, they'll end up killing them. And they've stacked the deck against you. What they don't know is that I've shuffled the cards."

"And the deck is no longer stacked?"

"No, it's still stacked, just in your favor now."

* * *

 Shannon drove to Richmond and arrived just before dark. She quickly found the park mentioned by Charlie and parked nearby. She observed the park from surrounding streets for nearly an hour before she saw a man walking Marley. She watched as he slowly marched Marley through the park for an hour and then the pair left the park with Shannon trailing behind them. Shannon watched as they walked several blocks from the center of the town and then entered an old warehouse. She retreated to her car and circled the area around the warehouse. She parked her car and made her way to an abandoned building near the warehouse where she could observe the building.

 It was nearly another hour before Marley was led from the building by the man she'd seen walking him earlier. Shannon focused on the activity at the warehouse and was relieved to see no one leaving the warehouse before or afterward. Whoever was walking Marley was either alone, or had surveillance in place in the park already with no one following him.

 Shannon left the abandoned building and walked towards the park. She saw the man sitting on a park bench with Marley sitting nearby looking bored. Shannon gave a low whistle and watched as Marley pricked his ears at the sound of her whistle. She gave another whistle and Marley jerked the leash from the hands of the man holding him and took off towards her. Within seconds Marley was all over Shannon and it took some time for her to calm the dog.

 "Easy, big fella!" said Shannon as the dog covered her in wet kisses. "Down! We've got some work to do Marley."

 "I take it you're Sara?" asked the man who had been handling the dog-sitting as he caught up with Marley.

 Shannon nodded and after taking a glance to be certain others weren't converging on them and said, "And I assume you're the guy Charlie told me about."

 "I'm one of them. Let's get out of here. There are some people around the area who we don't necessarily want to see you. We've got a facility nearby where we're headquartered. Let's head there and I can brief you on what we've found. You don't mind walking him?"

 "Marley's an old friend of mine," said Shannon petting the large shaggy head. "He's no trouble."

 Shannon, with Marley walking proudly alongside her, followed the man back to the warehouse she'd surveyed earlier. As they neared it Shannon could see a man rise from the doorway and open a door behind him. He held the door open and the man leading her gave him a nod as they walked past. Shannon followed the man upstairs to the second floor and then into a large room with cots around the perimeter and what looked like nine or ten men scattered about the room. In the center of the room was a large table covered with maps and photographs with cubicle walls with still more photos on them.

"Welcome to command central," said the man. "These men are my team and we're at your disposal. I've been told you'll want to know what we know about where the Underwoods are being held. Is that where you'd like to start?"

"It sounds good to me," said Shannon.

The man led the way to the large table and opened up a large map.

"We're here," he said pointing to a spot on the map. "Your friends are being held here." He pointed to a spot on the map several miles away.

"This was an old Bentley Security training facility. They'd abandoned it a couple of years ago. About ten days ago they started resuming activity there. Holes in the security fencing were patched. New security cameras were installed. They added various sensors and whatnot to the perimeter fencing. The buildings in the center of the compound were cleaned out and furnished. Back behind those buildings are still more structures that are impossible to see from the road. People started to take up residence there and we now believe about fifty people are living there.

"In these satellite photos, you can see the perimeter fencing. It maintains about a one-mile perimeter around the facility. Inside that there's another security fence about three hundred yards from the main buildings. Bentley security people are patrolling the space between those two fences around the clock. They're patrolling in three shifts with some reserve forces waiting back here in town should they be needed."

"Are those helicopters?" asked Shannon looking closely at the photographs and pointing to two objects hidden behind the buildings.

"Two of them," said the man. "They also have three armored vehicles in addition to a small fleet of other vehicles. The interesting thing is they have everything set up so that anyone without access to the satellite photos would think there was minimal force guarding the facility. They're trying to lure you out into the open only to open up on you and capture or kill you."

"That's cheery," said Shannon.

"It would be easier to break into Fort Knox than this place. Are you sure it's worth it?"

"Are you sure my friends are in there?"

"They're there," said the team leader. "Bentley's guys are relying on wireless microphones and cameras to monitor them. We've intercepted the feeds and are monitoring things. They're there and they're doing okay for now. They know that their survival is temporary though. We've heard Celia worrying that they let her see their faces so she's pretty much sure that they're going to get killed unless someone saves them."

"Then it's worth it. Let me take some time to absorb all of this and come up with some sort of a plan."

"We've got a scenario we're pretty comfortable with if you'd like to take a look at it."

"I want to do this alone if possible."

"It's not possible," said the team leader. "Like it or not, you need us."

"I can't ask your team to take this kind of a chance. I'm not sure I could live with myself if this went bad."

"If this goes bad you won't have to worry about living with it for long," joked the team leader. "Bentley's team has set this up to stop a one-person attack. They are geared up to stop you. They don't know that we're here. They've covered all of their bases and there's no way a single-person attack could succeed. What they don't know is that we're here and we're able to turn this thing around so the advantage is on your side."

"I don't want anyone else getting hurt."

"You don't have to worry about us. This is what we do. These men have been in the line of fire dozens of times already and faced tougher odds than this. We all know what could happen and we've all long ago accepted the odds. If you want to get your friends out, then you're going to need us."

"Let's see this plan of yours."

* * *

This night had been exactly like every other night since Harold Smick had been sent here from Bentley Security headquarters. For eight hours he would stand in the cold and stare into nothingness waiting for some mystery woman to appear so he or one of his colleagues could capture or kill her. Unlike every other night though, something was happening tonight. The headlights of a car were coming down the road towards his gate. The four men at this post tensed as the car approached and all touched their weapons for reassurance.

There had been a few cars coming down the road since they'd set up the position, but nearly all had been during the daylight and had simply been lost drivers. Now at three o'clock in the morning, Harold's instincts told him this was different. The car stopped about twenty feet from the gate and Harold walked towards the driver's side door while his partner walked towards the passenger side door. As he neared the car the driver reached up and flipped on the cabin light illuminating the interior of the car. The face of the woman he'd been told to expect smiled back at him from behind the windshield.

He raised his weapon and shouted, "Shut off the engine and step out of the car!"

The girl gave him the finger and revved the car's engine. Harold fired off a volley of shots at the head of the woman. As his shots rang out there was no doubt in his mind that his aim had been true. Even the car suddenly moving forward caused him no undue alarm. He assumed her foot had simply slipped off the brake when she'd died. As he watched the car move by him it suddenly became clear that the bullets had not penetrated the windshield and that the driver was anything but dead.

He raised his weapon again and fired off the remainder of the clip as the car surged forward and crashed through the security gate and past the first line of perimeter fencing. He could see his shots impacting the car, but the car didn't stop or veer off course. The four men emptied their weapons at the departing vehicle and then hurried off down the road in pursuit.

* * *

Shannon had been extraordinarily pleased to find that the bullet-resistant glass had performed as advertised. Her little red sports car was built more like a tank than a sports car and it readily absorbed the impact with the gate and surged forward as those she'd just passed fired after her vehicle. Shannon mashed the gas pedal and sped through the second perimeter fence and towards the buildings in the compound. Men were hurrying from the buildings as she drove into the area. Shannon heard more shots impacting her car as she sped in a circle around the compound and then sped back off along the road she'd taken in.

As she drove off, she could hear the helicopters being fired up. The men she'd passed on the way in were now in her path on the way out. She drove through them as they fired upon her car again as she raced towards them and they dove for cover as she drove past.

Shannon checked her rearview mirror and was not surprised to see multiple vehicles pulling out to pursue her. Leading the charge was an armored personnel carrier followed closely by two others. Shannon raced back towards the gate that she'd smashed through on her way into the compound.

* * *

The helicopter pilots had been annoyed to be kept on constant alert in the helicopters, but as soon as the first word of a possible intrusion reached them they had the engines started and warming up. By the time Shannon had completed her lap around the facility, the first helicopter had been ready to fly with the second one just a few seconds behind it. The pilot of the lead helicopter was now closing in on Shannon as she approached the gate she'd crashed through earlier. He slewed the helicopter sideways so that the open door with the machine gun positioned in it had a clear field of fire at Shannon's car. The gunner was just about to open up when an alarm sounded in the pilot's headset.

"What the hell?" were the last words of the pilot as the shoulder-launched surface-to-air missile blew the first helicopter out of the sky. The second helicopter pilot saw the missile attack and pulled his helicopter into a tight turn to the left away from the firing point of the first missile only to find a second missile rising from this location and impacting his helicopter.

* * *

Those in the armored vehicles saw the helicopters get hit and after a brief hesitation, they continued in pursuit of Shannon. All three armored vehicles disappeared in flames as three anti-tank shoulder-launched missiles hit them. The other vehicles pursuing Shannon were now blocked by the burning vehicles and truth be told, their hearts were no longer in the pursuit. They slowed to a stop and several of the vehicles tried to turn around and head back to the relative safety of the compound when the first mortar rounds struck the position. Several cars exploded with the first impact and several others were disabled. The surviving pursuers were now in full survival mode and they rapidly abandoned their vehicles to find themselves in the open and exposed facing an unknown enemy with unknown capabilities. It was now that the snipers started picking them off.

To those now being hunted the shots seemed to be coming from every direction, but there was no target to return fire at. Mortars continued to rain down on clusters of men and individuals were being picked off by the snipers. There was no safety. Return fire was aimed randomly while the fire from the attackers was deadly accurate. The assault lasted just minutes before the men who had been pursuing Shannon started to throw down their weapons and raise their arms in surrender.

* * *

The Underwood's had been asleep when the assault had started. The sound of distant gunshots had reached them first, then the sound of the vehicle racing through the compound followed by the helicopters taking off and more vehicles racing off followed by more distant gunshots and explosions.

"What's going on?" asked the kids worriedly as their parents tried to shield them. "Is someone coming to help us?"

Loud explosions echoed through the compound before either could reply and the two parents used their bodies to shield their children. More distant gunshots could be heard and still more explosions before the noise finally abated. Finally, a car could be heard approaching the building and the Underwoods turned their attention to the door as they could hear someone approaching it.

"Hi guys," said Shannon as she opened the door and slid into the room.

"Thank, God!" muttered Celia.

"How?" asked Tommy Underwood.

"It's a long story and we've got to get you guys out of here," said Shannon. "The guys who were holding you have reinforcements not too far away. We caught them by surprise this time, but they're going to be pissed and it's better for all of us if we're not here when they get here."

A man came in behind Shannon and she stood aside as he examined the door on the prison cell.

"Not a problem," said the man as he reached into his bag and removed a small object. He pressed it against the lock and then looked to the Underwoods and nodded towards the back of the cell before saying, "You might want to step back a bit while I blow the lock off this thing."

The two parents shielded their kids once more and then with a loud pop the charge removed the lock and the man swung open the cell door. All four Underwoods raced from the cell with Celia stopping to embrace Shannon.

"There's an armored car outside to take you guys someplace safe," said Shannon. "I want you to stay there until this is all done. I've got another week or two of work to finish up and then you should be safe. These guys will be keeping you safe until I get done. Don't argue, just do it."

Celia looked like she desperately wanted to know more, but she finally just nodded and said "Thanks" before following the men out to the armored car.

* * *

The team leader watched as his men secured the facility and then found Shannon standing nearby.

"How are they?"

"Shaken but okay," said Shannon. "You guys did a good job."

"We're not done yet," said the team leader.

"The rest of this job is mine."

"You'll need our help. My men and I are more than ready to finish this with you."

Shannon looked at the man and slowly shook her head.

"This has gotten personal and it has to end. I'm ending this. Just keep the Underwoods safe. I've got the rest of this. I appreciate the help though."

* * *

Craig Burke had just been waking up when the call came in. He sat on the edge of the bed as the caller briefed him on the few details he had available.

"Shannon showed up to rescue her friends as expected, but she didn't come alone. It looks like she brought a substantial force with her."

"Did we get her?"

"No. She got away and she took the Underwoods with her."

"Son of a bitch!" muttered Craig acidly. "How did she do it?"

"From the reports I've heard, it sounds like thirty or more men were involved. Our survivors report taking coordinated fire from multiple directions. The helicopters were taken out as were the armored vehicles. They had anti-aircraft and anti-armor capabilities along with mortars. This was a military operation."

"Our military?" asked Craig.

"No," said the adviser. "I've checked with all of our sources and all of the United States forces are present and accounted for. This was either a foreign operation or mercenaries."

"Where is she now?"

"We don't know. Our reserve forces responded as soon as they got word, but by the time they'd arrived the others were gone. They're treating the survivors and interviewing them now. We're looking at whatever tracking data we can find, but none of it is very helpful yet. The attackers were all dressed in black and masked. We're still in the very preliminary stages of this. We should know more in the next few hours. The cover story we're using to explain this is a training exercise gone wrong. If the Underwoods show up anyplace and tell their side though, we could have some bigger issues."

"We've got to find them and prevent that."

* * *

Shannon said her final goodbyes to the Underwoods back at the factory and then watched as they were loaded into an armored vehicle for a trip to a remote airstrip. One of Charlie's private jets was waiting to take them all to a nice safe location until this all ended.

"You guys did a good job," said Shannon appreciably to the men who were now celebrating their victory.

"We've got to get moving," said their commander. "Bentley didn't know we were around before, but they're going to flood this area with people now looking for us. We're well enough hidden to avoid detection short term, but they'd find us pretty soon if we stayed here for long. We'll get your friends someplace nice and safe for a while. Are you sure you don't need our help anymore?"

"No," said Shannon. "I'll deal with this myself. It may take a few days, but this ends."

* * *

"She has help now?" muttered the President getting the briefing from Craig Burke.

"It looks like she had a small military unit working with her. Our forensics guys are still going over everything, but that's how it looks now. The initial report was thirty to fifty attackers, but it now looks more like it was ten to twelve. They had anti-aircraft and anti-tank weapons. Mostly Russian-made stuff. They had snipers and mortar launchers. We weren't prepared to handle what they threw at us. They had good intelligence about our capabilities and they knew how to neutralize our capabilities."

"Who were they?"

"I don't know. They were well-trained professionals operating with good coordination. The best guess is mercenaries, but we haven't heard of anyone hiring mercenaries. Russians maybe since the weapons were mostly Russian. This situation just got ten times more dangerous."

"What happened with the Underwoods?"

"They were removed and appear to be unharmed. We don't know where they are now. We intercepted a cell phone call that Celia Underwood made about a half-hour after the event where she called her mother to tell her that everyone was fine but that they were disappearing for a while and not to worry. We went to the site where that call originated, but no one was there. The cell phone that was used was there, but that's it. It was purchased in a nearby drug store a few days earlier and activated but not used until then. We're looking into that to see if we can find out who bought it."

"What happens now?"

"Now we pray she makes a big mistake," said Craig. "She's been a handful on her own and now with this force behind her, there's no safety for anyone she considers an enemy. Even the White House isn't safe against this type of force. If that force were to storm the White House in a well-coordinated attack there's a reasonably good chance they could get to you before they could be stopped.

"I think we can also safely assume Roger is dead unless we can get him out of prison and someplace safe," said Craig. "We were able to hide him there for the short term by getting him moved to the infirmary, but they'll be moving him back to his normal cell in another day or two and he's vulnerable there. We can't protect him in prison against that kind of force and she can kill him anytime she wants to. I'm not sure we can protect him anyplace else, but he's a sitting duck in prison. I've got people in the area around the prison providing extra security but they can't deal with that kind of a force. He's dead if we leave him there."

"There isn't a lot I can do to help him."

"You could pardon him."

"Pardoning him would be political suicide," muttered Hector. "I'm not even sure I can pardon someone unless they're accused of a federal crime."

"You can order him released. The Constitution gives you pretty broad power. The courts have tried to rein it in a bit, but you could order him released and we could get him out of the area before the courts could intervene. My sources say the party will back you on this. If you don't get him out of jail, then he's dead. I can't protect him in prison. No one can. The party will rally around you if you pardon him, but if he dies in prison then things could get tricky. You know he didn't kill Mimi. We all know he didn't kill Mimi. Justice is best served by setting him free. Not only justice, but you'd save his life."

"The press has already convicted him," countered Hector. "They'll come down on me like a ton of bricks. Why don't we have the governor pardon him?"

"Governor Small is up for reelection. The pardon would likely doom his campaign. You're safe for three years. This will all be a dim memory by then."

"The press will kill me."

"There are things that can be done to distract them. I wouldn't worry about the press too much. The public has a short memory and it's a long time until you need the public's support again. This will be a distant memory by then."

"Can you take him out of prison?"

"By force?" asked Craig. Hector nodded.

"Sure. But that would be even more problematic. He'd be a wanted man and have to find a place to lie low. We'd likely have to kill a few people in the process and there would be all kinds of issues raised. It would be quickly linked to you whether you played a role in it or not. I can organize it, but we'd have to have a haven that would be out of reach and I'm not sure such a place exists. It's just not practical to forcibly remove him."

"Why didn't we just leave her alone?" muttered Hector.

"We can sit here for days debating what could have, should have happened, but the reality is we're here and we have to move forward from here."

"So I have to pardon Roger?"

"If you want him to live we have to get him out of prison. The judge won't set bail so the only way to get him out is to pardon him, or physically remove him. A pardon is the best option."

"I'll take care of it. What happens after that?"

"We're going to have to do this quietly and get him out of sight as quickly as possible. We've got his island home equipped to withstand anything Shannon is likely to throw at it. Everything there has been enhanced so he should be safe if we can get him there. Once he's free we'll pick him up in an armored truck and keep him surrounded by body armor. He'll go straight to his jet and head for the island. If we can keep this all quiet for just a few hours, then he should be safe. Once he's safe then we'll work on finding Shannon and ending this. She can't hide forever. She's been incredibly lucky so far, all it takes is one stroke of bad luck and we'll have her."

* * *

It took a while for the paperwork to be processed. The Attorney General was unhappy with the pardon, but the pardon was issued and at one in the morning a series of vehicles pulled up to the gates of the prison. Dozens of highly armed Bentley security guards patrolled the nearby woods looking for anyone who didn't belong. Roger Bentley was shrouded in layers of bullet-resistant clothing and raced from the prison gates to the back doors of an armored car. A convoy of vehicles then surrounded the armored car and raced from the area. The trip to the airport where two of Roger's private jets had been flown took only twenty minutes, but they were the longest twenty minutes of Craig Burke's life.

"You can relax," said Roger Bentley. "No one knows I'm getting out. No one knows where I'm going. As good as Shannon Brewer is, she isn't that good."

"I've learned not to underestimate that girl," said Craig Burke. "When you're in the air and out of her reach, I'll relax, but until then I'm not relaxing."

"How is the security at the island?"

"We've replaced all of the windows with bullet-resistant glass. We've built a blast wall around the compound. We've quadrupled the number of guards. We've got every sensor known to mankind in place along with trained dogs. No one moves on that island without me knowing about it. Once we get you there you should be safe. It's getting you there safely that has me worried."

"You worry too much. She's good, but she's not God."

The convoy entered the airport and drove directly to a heavily guarded hangar. The hangar doors were closed and secured before Craig would let Roger out of the armored truck. Two jets were parked inside the hangar along with two crews.

"You know there's just one of me right?" asked Roger Bentley eyeing the jets.

"I'm sending up a decoy first. If she's out there I want to find out before I put you in the air. Let's get you into the plane."

Roger climbed aboard the plane and watched out the window as the hangar doors were opened and the convoy drove out followed by the first jet. The jet taxied out to the runway and paused, awaiting clearance. Craig had security people all around the airport and no one reported any suspicious activity. The plane was cleared for takeoff and taxied down the runway. At the end of the runway, the pilot pulled back on the stick and the plane flew off without incident.

"Like I said," said Roger Bentley. "She's not God. She's dangerous, but we're smarter and better than she is. She's been lucky so far, but her luck will run out."

"I've learned not to underestimate her. She may not be superwoman, but she's the closest thing to one I've ever found. "

"Are you coming with me?"

"No. I'm staying behind to coordinate our efforts to find her. You're not going to be safe and none of the rest of us will be safe until that girl is dead and buried."

The doors to the second jet were closed and the hangar doors reopened. The jet taxied out onto the runway awaiting clearance. When the clearance came the pilot opened up the throttle and the jet lunged forward. At the end of the runway, the pilot pulled back on the controls and the plane lifted off the runway and into the sky.

Craig Burke was just breathing a sigh of relief when the distant report from a rifle stopped him. He looked to the jet that was still moving upwards and watched in horror as it rolled over and fell from the sky. The fireball that erupted upon impact made it all too clear that there would be no survivors.

His men were fanning out to find the shooter but Craig had no doubt who it had been. He stood frozen in the doorway of the hangar waiting for the shot that was meant for him, but it never came. Instead, radio calls started coming back of finding the shooting spot, but no one was there. Craig called for roadblocks to be placed, but he had little hope that they'd find Shannon. She was always a step ahead of them. He rode over to the burning wreckage with the firefighters. The cockpit had not yet been engulfed in flames and he could see the hole in the left side of the cockpit window where Shannon's fifty caliber slug had entered, gone through the heads of both pilots and then the matching hole on the right side where it had left the plane after doing its job.

Despite it all, he had to admire the marksmanship. Firing a single shot from nearly a mile away at a rapidly moving target and hitting and killing both pilots was incredibly good. Maybe, just maybe Shannon Brewer was superwoman.

* * *

Back in Montana, the Underwoods had been escorted to a safe house near Charlie's main house. The men who had freed them were now providing security for them, yet Celia felt far from safe. Being kidnapped from her home and held hostage had injured her in a way that no physical injury possibly could.

"I hate this," muttered Celia.

"It won't be for long," said Tommy. "We'll be able to go home in a few days."

"I don't want to go home. I can't go home. They stole home from me. I used to think I was safe there. I used to think I could look after the kids and keep them safe. They stole that from me. I know how dirty things are back there now and I don't want to go back."

"What do you want to do?" asked Tommy.

"I don't know. But I can't go back home. I just can't. I can't take the chance of that happening again."

Tommy Underwood looked at his wife and knew how she felt. As sheriff, he'd always felt in control. When things spiraled out of control it fell to him to restore order. He always knew what to say or do, but now he was at a loss. He now knew that those in political power had played a role in all of this and whatever trust he'd had in politicians and the political system was now gone. He now knew that his survival and the survival of his family depended on the whims of politicians who had shown they could care less.

"So what do we do?" asked Tommy.

"I don't know. I don't want to become a crazy recluse hiding in a cabin in the woods, but I'm starting to understand their view. I don't know what to do. I just want to be safe and to know my kids are safe."

* * *

Newsrooms around the country received a package containing a DVD. It wasn't long before the DVD was playing on television stations all over the country.

"My name is Janet Mills and I'm a contract killer," said the silhouetted image of a young woman. "Lately people have known me as Shannon Brewer. I've gone by many aliases during my life. Six years ago I retired from the business and I thought I had put that stage of my life behind me. I was wrong. I married, had a child, and was living a normal life. Then an attempt was made on my life that killed both my husband and son and left me wounded. This attack upon me was launched by Bentley Security to prevent the information I'm about to disclose from ever becoming public.

"Over ten years ago Hector Esteban contacted me to kill his wife Gabrielle. He had started a relationship with his current wife Carol Bentley and didn't want the political fallout that could harm his political career were he to divorce Gabrielle. He had learned from a mutual acquaintance of my capabilities and contacted me. Here is the video of that first meeting."

The video then showed the meeting between the two discussing what needed to be done and then concluded with Hector handing over the one hundred thousand dollars and the keys to his house and the code to the alarm system.

That portion of the video ended and the next thing on the DVD showed a shaky image as a camera was being carried and then set down. When the image stabilized it showed Gabrielle lying on the bed, apparently sound asleep with her mouth open and snoring.

A silhouetted figure approached the bed with a syringe with a long fine needle on it. She lifted Gabrielle's arm and applied a tourniquet. Gabrielle shuffled a bit on the bed but didn't awaken. Shannon then slid the very fine needle into a vein and drew back on the syringe and blood flowed into the syringe mixing with the drug within it. Shannon loosened the tourniquet and then slid the plunger forward on the syringe. The drug flowed into Gabrielle's body. Shannon pulled back on the syringe to put some blood back in the syringe then removed the hair-like needle and applied pressure over the site for a few seconds. Gabrielle continued to sleep through all of this. Then within a minute or two, Gabrielle gave a small twitch or two, and then her breathing slowed and finally stopped. Shannon rose from the bed and walked back towards the camera and the video ended.

"We next met when Hector learned I was back in town and he assumed I was planning on blackmailing him. He sent four thugs to kill me."

The video now switched to the back of the Mazza brothers' truck where a beaten and tortured Victor Mazza told Sara who had hired them.

"I then paid Hector a visit," said Sara.

Next came the later video showing Hector standing at the foot of the bed while Sara held him at gunpoint. He confessed to sending the Mazza's after Sara and agreed to never target her again.

"I thought my dealings with Hector were done at that time. I left the west coast and moved east. I gave up my old life and met a wonderful man. I settled into the role of wife and mother and put my past behind me. For the next five years, I led a perfectly normal life. I had no intention of ever returning to my previous occupation, or doing anything other than being as good a wife and mother as I could be.

"When Hector decided to run for President it was determined that the information I held and that you've now seen posed too great a threat to his presidency. A massive effort was launched to find me, and those hunting me succeeded. They found where I was living. They tracked me. They filmed me as I went about my daily business. They ambushed my husband, son, and me as we were out for a drive. We were forced from the road and Bentley Security gunmen opened fire, killing my husband and son and wounding me. I was able to elude them and escape.

"I later found eight of those who had participated in the attack on my family and killed them. I then retreated for a while to heal, both mentally and physically. I heard from some sources that Bentley Security was still actively hunting for me. They would not let this drop. They declared war on me and I ultimately ended up engaging them in that war. A while ago I brought about the death of Mimi Bentley and planted evidence to make it clear that Roger Bentley was the killer.

"I approached Bentley Security and made it clear that I would exonerate Roger Bentley and end the war in exchange for a cash payout. Both sides had lost enough life and it was time for this to end. I was told that Hector would not accept such a deal and that he felt safe in the White House. I then attempted to remind Hector of how unsafe he truly was."

Shannon then played a tape showing the Esteban children, Carol Esteban, and finally Hector Esteban in the sights of her rifle. The video ended with the shot into the then-empty chair of Hector Esteban right after he'd risen.

"After this message was sent to Hector I expected him to comply and call off the attacks against me, but it wasn't to be. A family that I'd been close to was kidnapped by Bentley Security agents. They were held in a heavily guarded compound to trap me and kill me. With the help of a few friends I was able to raid that compound and free my friends who are now safe and in hiding and kill most of those who were holding them hostage."

"I've been hunted by Bentley Security to prevent me from showing you what you've now seen. They've consistently refused to call off the war when given multiple opportunities. They've expanded the attacks to former friends of mine. I have little hope that exposing this tape will lead to a cessation of the attacks against me, but it's time the American people knew the truth.

"I've done some bad things in my past. During my days as an assassin, I killed people who didn't deserve to die. I did my job quickly and efficiently. I killed the majority of my victims as painlessly and humanely as possible. The exceptions were rare. I knew the risks I took and the potential for trouble down the road. The videos you've seen were made to use as leverage in case someone came after me.

"Someone has now come after me. He's responsible for the death of my husband and son. He's responsible for the deaths of those men he hired to track me down and kill me. He's responsible for the kidnapping of Sheriff Tommy Underwood and his family. He's the President of the United States, Hector Esteban."

The video then showed a table containing various items. She continued her presentation.

"This syringe is the syringe that was used to drug Gabrielle Esteban. There should be adequate DNA evidence in and on it to verify that this syringe was used in the video you've just watched. This vial contains the remnants of the chemical that was used to bring about Gabrielle Esteban's death. All of this and more including the original videos are being placed in a storage facility whose location is being disclosed to the proper authorities.

"I've been very patient and willing to compromise, but Hector Esteban and Bentley Security have refused to back down. It's time America knew the truth. Hector Esteban is not worthy of the job that he has been entrusted with."

* * *

The new head of the party met with Hector to discuss his future.

"I won't resign," said Hector.

"You don't have a choice. If you don't step down then you'll be removed. We need you to step aside."

"Son of a bitch! You're letting her bring me down?"

"You brought yourself down. We need to hold the presidency. You're going to be charged with murder. Your best bet would be to take some sort of a plea deal. The party would prefer this not end with a trial, so a plea deal is in everyone's best interest."

"I can fight and win the case. The video has to be substantiated and unless Sara comes forward, it can't be used against me. She won't come forward so it can't be used in court."

"You can't take this to trial. We can't allow that. The cost to the party would be too high. It's already been too high. We don't need everything that happened here to be rehashed in the courts. We want this finished as quickly as possible. Admit what you did, confess to your crime, and take a plea deal."

"You don't care if I end up in prison?"

"I have to look out for the party, first and foremost. I'd prefer you didn't have to be inconvenienced, but I can't sacrifice the party for you."

"I've devoted my life to the party and this is how I get repaid?"

"You've made mistakes that have damaged the party. We've lost Roger as a result of your mistakes. He and Mimi paid with their lives for your earlier mistake of killing Gabrielle. Too many people have died to have this end without someone taking the fall."

"And what if I fight it out? What if I refuse to resign or accept a plea?"

"Then you'll be dealt with."

"What does that mean?"

"Let's not get into unpleasantness. You should talk with your wife and advisers and then step aside. Take the plea and serve your time. The vice president will take over and things should quiet down pretty quickly."

* * *

The world watched with fascination as the President of the United States resigned from office and was immediately placed into custody for the murder of his first wife. The press had a field day and his arrest dominated the news coverage. The prosecutor initially refused to speculate on a plea deal, but within a few days, a plea deal was reached where Hector Esteban would serve seven years in prison and then an extended period of probation and public service afterward. Many on the right felt the deal was overly generous, but the problems of prosecuting someone with the evidence available made this the best deal possible for all parties.

* * *

Four years later.

"Are you ready to go man?" asked the prison guard.

"I'm so ready to go," said Hector Esteban.

The prison sentence of seven years had been reduced as a result of good behavior and prison overcrowding, so Hector was being released after serving just over half of his sentence. This would be his last day in prison. He'd awakened at three in the morning and packed his belongings. His nightmare was now on the verge of ending. His attorney had a couple of book deals under consideration for him that would provide him with substantial income and his life could resume. It would be different than it had been, but life would go on.

He picked up his bags and followed the guard as he led him from the cellblock where Hector had spent the last three years. They made their way out of the cellblock and started to cross a small open area leading to the administration building where the paperwork would be completed and Hector would then be free to go.

As he was about to enter the building Hector thought he felt someone punch him in the chest. Both bags fell from his hands and he looked down to see the front of his shirt turning red from the blood pouring from the gunshot wound. He buckled to his knees as the guards ran around the area attempting to find the shooter, but it was impossible. There was no one in sight. Hector fell onto his side and died as more guards swarmed the yard.

* * *

Sara watched through the rifle sight until she was confident that Hector was dead. A second round was in the chamber in case it was necessary, but a single fifty caliber bullet to the chest had been more than adequate. She slid the rifle into its case and made her way back to the street. The gun was replaced into the gun case hidden in the frame of the car and she then climbed into the driver's seat. She pulled away from the curb and started to head out of the city.

Once she was some distance away she pulled out her cellular phone and made her call.

"It's done," said Shannon into the phone.

"I was just watching on television," said Craig Burke. "That was a hell of a shot."

"I've made harder shots. I trust this will make your sponsors happy?"

"I think the party would have been happier if you'd killed him before this whole mess started, but this is the best-case scenario given where we were. Did you have any trouble?"

"No. Things went fine. The investigators should be able to link this to Roger's slaying and the earlier shot at the White House so that should keep the focus off Bentley. They'll be looking at me for this, but I'm not that easy to find."

"Are you retiring again, or can I call you from time to time?"

"You can call, but I can't guarantee I'll take the job. If the case is right, and the payday is right I'll consider it, but I don't need the money anymore."

Craig Burke smiled at that. The ten million that Bentley Security had just given Shannon Brewer to prevent Hector's tell-all book would just about guarantee anyone's financial security. Add in the fifty million or so he suspected she had stashed from her earlier jobs and Shannon Brewer was possibly one of the wealthiest people Craig Burke knew. He had no doubt she was the most dangerous person he knew.

"Be careful out there," said Craig. "I need you alive."

"I'm always careful," said Shannon. She ended the call and tossed the phone out the window of the car and watched in the rearview mirror as a truck behind her crushed the phone under its tires.

Author's Notes

If you enjoyed the book, then help me out by spreading the word. Word of mouth is vital to any author. Word of mouth is the best advertising any author could hope to get. Thanks for reading this and I hope you enjoyed it!

Made in United States
North Haven, CT
09 December 2025